DANGEROUS MYTHS
OF THE WESTERN WORLD

Dangerous Myths
of the
Western World

Richard Malmed

KS

Kravitz & Sons

INNOVATORS IN PUBLISHING, MARKETING AND ADVERTISING

Kravitz and Sons LLC
1301 Farmville Blvd, Suite 104
Greenville, NC 27834

Published by Kravitz and Sons LLC.
ISBN: 979-8-89639-125-8 (sc)
ISBN: 979-8-89639-124-1 (e)

Library of Congress Control Number: 2025904111

Contents

THE *Two* MARYS

RICHARD MALMED

The two Marys of the New Testament, the mother of Jesus and the Magdalene, are each an enduring Christian myth and folk totem, that have not only become icons but have increased in importance and influence in the Christian community over the centuries. Yet none of their attributes are based on historical evidence nor can withstand forensic or historical scrutiny. And each has been detrimental to the feminine population of the west and held it in virtual servitude for over 1,900 years. One is a two dimensional passive virgin, the other a whore. Only now are women emerging from the deleterious effects of these myths.

As an arm of the state, from Constantine onward at the direction of the emperors, the Christian church began to become organized into a hierarchy with departments and divisions which mirrored the structure of the Roman army and its municipal or state government. Prior to Constantine, the various Christian churches could and did expound a number of variations of Christianity, with the different bishops having little control over the priests of the congregations. People could seek out congregations to fit their beliefs. After the Nicean conference in 325 C.E., the monolithic power structure could exert tremendous pressure on the priests to keep their teachings in line with both the orthodox religion, but also the political leanings of the secular government. For at the least 1,000 years, secular rulers controlled the church and used it to advance their personal ambitions or that of their dynasties' to conquer or dominate neighboring segments, extract tribute or murder, plunder, enslave or otherwise control populations.

Mother MARYS

RICHARD MALMED

In the actual gospels, Mary the mother of Jesus appears rarely and only in a limited role. In perhaps the most influential role, she is deemed to have, as a virgin, given birth to Jesus following her impregnation by the Holy Spirit. She appears at the marriage of Cana where, in the Gospel of John 2:1, she encourages perhaps Jesus' first miracle. And later, she appears at Jesus' crucifixion, but not at the discovery of the empty tomb subsequently. Yet Mary has come to be an object of worship on a par with Jesus, while surpassing the God the father figure and the Holy Spirit. Non-canonical myths have her being assumed into heaven in human form in a manner similar to that of Jesus.

The marriage of Cana appearing only in the Gospel of John 1:1-11 is an intriguing glimpse into the character of Mary. In the scene, Mary complains to Jesus that the wedding party is running out of wine. In one of his first apparent miracles, Jesus changes water into wine and saves the host of the wedding from social embarrassment. The inclusion in the Gospel raises many questions and areas for speculation. The first and most obvious question is whose wedding is it? If the responsibility to provide wine falls on the host, and Mary complains to Jesus, then Jesus must be in some sense, the host. Does that mean that either Mary, Jesus or one of Jesus' brothers is the bridegroom? Could Jesus be marrying Mary Magdalene – as many speculate? Certainly, by this time, Jesus is grown and answerable to the wedding guests for their wine. Joseph does not appear in the story at all and must be presumed to be dead or he would have been responsible for the wine. If so, Mary is no longer marriageable, even without her brood of at least four sons. Nonetheless, we see Mary fulfilling her role as a responsible matron of the Galilean community in Cana, and well aware of her social position and responsibilities. This is a pleasant, human portrait of a grown woman nagging her now grown son. Overall, however, the incident must be considered a somewhat trivial event – with all the problems Jesus must face in his new ministry, why would wine for a bunch of wedding imbibers be of such importance that it appears in a gospel other than to portray Jesus performing a miracle?

In that context, the question must arise: Why would Jesus perform miracles for some and not others, why perform miracles for non-believing Romans or Samaritans and not exclusively Jews. In some cases, the miracles are preceded by good works, or strong assertions of devotion to God, but not others and lastly, the wine miracle is a well-known magic trick performed by false bottomed containers. Perhaps a clever performance for a gullible collection of wedding guests, but of little moral or religious value.

Virgin BIRTH

RICHARD MALMED

Only two of the Gospels, Matthew and the Luke, report the story of the virgin birth, while neither Mark, the documents attributed to Paul, Acts nor John make any such reference. It is important to understand the chronology of the different canonical documents. Jesus was crucified in the early 30s CE, and the Pauline letters et al. and Acts appear to have been written in the early 50s. Mark was written shortly thereafter. In the early 60s, James, Jesus' brother, was killed on the orders of Ananas, the high priest of the Temple. Matthew and Luke were written in the early 70s CE after the Romans put down a Jewish uprising and destroyed the Temple. John is perhaps written at least a generation later between the 90s and 110 CE. Scholars generally agree that Matthew and Luke were each heavily based on a source known as the Q document, the date of whose creation is unknown.

Since the report of a virgin birth was an undoubtedly earthshaking claim, it must be considered highly suspect Mark or Paul failed to include that in their narratives or assertions. It is also significant that the claim of a young girl to have been impregnated by a godlike figure would have received great notoriety in a small Galilean village. Certainly, it would have been known and celebrated during Jesus' lifetime and given him great stature and credibility. Yet virtually nothing is known of Jesus' life between his birth and his appearance in John the Baptist's entourage at the bank of the Jordan River thirty years later. There is a charming tale of Jesus as a boy meeting with wise men at the Temple in Jerusalem during one of his family's pilgrimages. While this is consistent with Jesus' later erudition during his ministry, it does not support the assertions of a virgin birth.

The Gospels themselves however contradict the notion of virgin birth. Jesus' lineage was supposedly traced back to David as part of his claim to being a messiah or the "King of the Jews." Both Luke and Matthew put forth long family trees tracing Jesus back to David, although each uses a different list of intermediate progenitors. Nonetheless, in each Gospel, the starting point for each retrospective tracing is Joseph – the husband of Mary, but, as per the Gospels asserting virgin birth, not the father of Jesus. If Mary were to have given birth to Jesus with the Holy Spirit as father, Joseph is obviously irrelevant to the bloodline, and, if asserted during Jesus' ministry, would have damaged any claim to the Jewish throne.

The Catholic Church for several centuries now has attempted to assert that Mary was always a virgin after the birth of Jesus. In the Gospels themselves, however Jesus' brothers are quite prominently referred to. His most esteemed brother was James the Just, widely renowned for his piety, who became the leader of the Jesus movement after his crucifixion. He is noteworthy for his disputes with Paul, whom he claimed perverted and obliterated many essential Jewish doctrines and practices. The Gospels note four brothers of Jesus, although there may have been a number of sisters. At the time, female children were not given the same status as males, so their existence was not recognized. At times, the Catholic Church apologists have suggested that Jesus' brothers were either cousins or half-brothers. Since there are specific words for either designation in Aramaic and Greek, it is unlikely that Gospel authors intended anything more or less than brother.

Yet John's Gospel dated about 30 to 50 years later does not mention the virgin birth, or any of the events claimed by Luke or Matthew such as Herod's murder of innocent children or the Bethlehem census.

Paul or whoever wrote Acts (probably an aide or assistant) while preaching in no uncertain terms the death and resurrection of Jesus, and his kinship with God the Father, never once referred to the virgin birth except to assert that he was God's son, a term often applied to all men and not necessarily implying a distinct father-son relationship.

From a purely forensic point of view, there would be two witnesses to the immaculate conception – the Holy Spirit and Mary herself. No reference ever appears of Mary making any such claim. The Holy Spirit does not appear to have communicated with any earthly being, his connection in any form of vision or otherwise. The sole reference is the Annunciation where Mary is told by an angel that she will be the woman to serve as the birth mother of God's child.

In the Jewish world, the idea of a virgin birth through the intercession of God or Yahweh would have been unthinkable and blasphemous. When the Jews accepted the belief of monotheism and began to see themselves as the covenanted people, the name of God was never used. He was considered to be so unknowable, so undefinable, that the very mention of his name was considered blasphemy – the punishment for which was death. He was considered to be an incorporeal spirit whose influences but not his actual physical being ever appeared in any scripture. Only his voice or some secondary evidence of his existence is seen in the burning bush, or his influence over military victories. He never assumed an anthropomorphic existence, i.e. one similar to the physical presence of man. For Yahweh, to have himself performed an act so human as to impregnate a young woman would be unthinkable. While the Greek or other pagan gods could easily have done so and frequently had, no such act could ever be attributable to God in Jewish theology. Such a concept could only have derived from later pagan influences.

On occasion, Christian theology in an effort to demonstrate its superior nature of Christianity over Judaism, points to references in the Old Testament and connects them to events in the life of Jesus and elsewhere. In this way they claim that the so-called Old Testament was a foreshadowing of the new religion based on Jesus. The main citation used to demonstrate this in the virgin birth is a reference to Isaiah 7:13. In that passage, it is mentioned in passing that a young woman (almah in Aramaic) will give birth to child whose name shall be "Immanuel." The term for virgin would have been "betulah" – an easily differentiated term to anyone familiar with Aramaic. Yet in Greek translation, the scribe mistranslated the term and, thus, gave rise to some substantiation for the virgin birth concept.

Perhaps the gap between the early 50s of the Markan Gospel and Paul's Letters and the Gospels of Matthew and Luke in the 70s or 80s CE explains the insertion of this essentially pagan idea. Two momentous events occurred in the Jewish community. In the early 60s, Festus, a somewhat incompetent Roman administrator of Judea and successor to Pontius Pilate was recalled to Rome, and left Judea without a strong Roman presence. Into that vacuum, the high priest of the Temple, Ananias, had James, Jesus' brother and the acknowledged and highly respected leader of the Jewish sect, killed in 62 CE. This assassination created a huge chasm between the emerging Christian community of Paul and the Jesus sect in Jerusalem. As will be explained later, Paul's followers were mostly pagan converts from Asia Minor and brought many pagan ideas into what was evolving as the Christian religion.

In the late 60s and early 70s, a Jewish uprising led to the Romans completely annihilating the population of Jerusalem and destroying the Temple. Jews and the essentially Jewish sect of the followers of Jesus were considered to be enemies of Rome.

For this reason, it was important for the now Pauline Christians of Asia Minor to distance themselves as much as possible from the political elements of the Jewish community. From that point forward, there were strong pagan influences in Paul's Christian religion and fewer Jewish ones. As a result the virgin birth concept took hold on very fertile ground among the pagan converts.

Assuming that Mary gave birth in insufficient time after her marriage to Joseph that the child would be deemed a product of premarital sex, this must have created a large problem not only for her but a major problem for the assembler of the Gospel narrative. A woman committing a premarital act of intercourse was often condemned in that time and that society. Joseph would certainly look like a fool for marrying her after she began to show. But to label Jesus a bastard would certainly be detrimental to his subsequent ministry. Why would the gospel writers include it in the narrative? In order to claim the miraculous virgin birth, the Gospel writers took a considerable risk by introducing the idea of Mary's impregnation prior to marriage, as an attribute of Jesus' image.

The miraculous birth myth was a highly popular technique for augmenting the status of the hero. Births by women well past child bearing years generally demonstrate that the child was a gift from God. Many figures in history and myth fall in this category among them: John the Baptist, Isaac and Caesar. Many pagan and especially Greek myths have a divine father impregnating a mortal female. This is very popular in Greek and Roman mythology and is found in other pagan cultures as well.

The Greek pantheon is replete with demigods or humans with male Gods as fathers. Zeus through a number of human females is father to Perseus (Danae), Theseus (Maria), Persephone (Demeter), Helen of Troy (Leda) and Pan is father of Hermes by a shepherdess.

In Persian culture, Zoroaster or Zarathustra is the product of a divine shaft of light and his birth mother Dughdova, Horus of Egypt is the product of Isis and the resurrection of her own dead husband Osiris. To the pagan world, a conception by a god with a human was not startling.

Perhaps, the most interesting and relevant miraculous births, are those of Vishnu in the Hindu religion and Buddha. Vishnu descended into the womb of Devaki and was reborn as her son Krishna, but Devaki herself was not a virgin; she already had seven children. Buddha in one of his incarnations entered the Queen Maya who was already married to the king. It had been speculated that several Greek myths arose about the time Alexander the Great conquered central Asia in 334 BCE and became conflated with the myths of Buddha. It is also noteworthy that what is referred to as "ayonija" means not born from the womb. This would bear a striking similarity to "Adonai." Adonai is the Hebrew word substituted for God, since Jews are forbidden to say the actual name of God. Adonis is a handsome Greek male god associated with annual dying and rebirth. The name Adonis is of prior pagan origin from this word "Adon" meaning god. Adonis has a strong sexual attribute in the attraction of women. As the Christian image of God began to emerge, the Hebraic Yahweh – an older, stern father figure – was replaced by a young virile male in his thirties, similar to Adonis.

The myth of chastity, purity and passivity of the Virgin Mary has had many deleterious effects in regard to women in the western world. Purity and virginity are essentially passive, nonproductive characteristics and, so women have been regarded. In contrast, the Old Testament has many contrary images of women. Certainly the Song of Songs depicts femininity in a vastly different way.

> Let him kiss me with the kisses of his mouth; for thy
> love is better than wine 1:2

> A bundle of myrrh is my beloved into me, he shall lie
> all night betwixt my breasts 1:13

> O my dove, that out in the clefts of the rock in the
> secret places of the stairs, let me see they countenance,
> let me hear thy voice, and thy countenance is comely.

1:14

Until the day break and the shadows flee away, turn,
my beloved, and be thou a roe or a young hart upon
the mountains of Bethel. 1:17

Thy breasts are like two roes that are twins which feed
upon the lilies 2:5

Let my beloved come into his garden and eat his
pleasant fruits 2:16

This section of the Old Testament is overwhelming with its sexual imagery and innuendo. Frequently the voice uttering this poetry is feminine.

It certainly is relevant that the works attributed to Paul or his followers are extremely misogynistic. In 1 Corinthians, Paul clearly advises his male followers not to marry.

"Those who marry will have an affliction to the flesh and I would spare you that." 1 Con 7.28

'He who marries a virgin does well and he who does not marry her does better." 7.38

"Women should remain silent in the churches. They are not allowed to speak, but must be in submission."

"If they want to inquire about something, they should ask their own husbands at home, for it is disgraceful for a woman to speak in church." 1 Cor. 14:35

These are from a document all scholars agree was written by Paul. In Timothy 2d, it is generally believed to be a follower or imitator of Paul. However, it is clearly in the collection of works of the New Testament. "I do not allow a woman to teach or exercise authority over a man." 1 Tim. 2:12

Yet if we compare this with Proverbs 31, we see that Jewish women, while still subordinate, are accorded great intelligence, and sophistication and given a wide range of familial and financial responsibilities. We have referred above to the Song of Songs to demonstrate the attitude toward sex in both men and women. It is important then to see in the canon of the New Testament harsh restrictions on women's sexuality, leadership and intellectual growth.

The Old Testament in contrast has many unique women with many nuances in character and temperament. Deborah was a judge who managed to stiffen the spine of her military leader Barak in one of the Bible's innumerable tribal battles. With her support and even physical presence, he won the confrontation. Jael, another female, beguiled the fleeing leader of the opposition into sleeping in her tent, and then nailed him through the temple with a tent spike. Another endearing story is that of Naomi and Ruth who, with a strong female bond, managed to survive the death of their husbands and navigate their way through troubled economic difficulties.

The Old Testament has many unique women. It is amazing that the writers of different parts of the Old Testament were able to portray such vibrant and colorful images of women in such sparse narratives. Yet we seem to sense the strong and complex character of these women even over the centuries. Sarah, Abraham's wife, deals with the embarrassment of being childless and then takes desperate measures to protect her son. Lot's daughters deal with facing the end of the human race and plot to ply their father with wine to secure his seed to continue human existence. Delilah's treachery is of course legendary.

Few figures in the New Testament have any characteristics outside of Peter and Paul, the other names are blank, even Jesus, Pontius Pilate, Joseph of Arimathea, Lazarus and others go begging for more imagery. But to consign Mary, Jesus mother and Mary Magdalene to bland matter-of-fact descriptions is even more startling, considering their stature in subsequent centuries.

Tamar

RICHARD MALMED

One of the most interesting stories of women is that of Tamar (Gen. 38). A man named Er was the first son of Judah, who procured for his son a wife named Tamar. When Er died, Judah told his second son Onan, to marry and impregnate her and dedicate the child to his first son as was then required by Levirate law. Instead of impregnating her he, "spilled his seed on the ground." (Incidentally, this verse Gen. 38:9 is the sole basis for some religions to ban masturbation and birth control). His motivation was that he did not want to "give seed to his brother." As a result, God punished him by death. Judah then sent her back to her father's house.

Under Jewish law, what Judah and his family had done was a major breach of law at the time. Each head of a family clan was charged with the responsibility to multiply, but also to take charge of and care for those members of his clan. Quite properly, Judah procured a wife for his son Er, who for an unknown reason, was wicked in the sight of the lord and died. Judah, as was the law necessary to preserve the family structure of his clan, ordered his son Onan to marry and impregnate Tamar. Without this marriage and a child, Tamar would be relegated to the status of a single old maid whose status in the clan would be essentially that of a servant. When Onan disobeyed his father and refused to give her a child, he was defaulting on a duty the clan owed to this woman. Under the Levirate law of the time, this child would get Er's inheritance and reduce Onan's share. Since Judah procured her for his son, it fell on the clan leader to make her a worthy and productive member of the clan. When he quite properly delegated his duty to his sons and they defaulted, it became his duty as clan leader to take care of her. When he defaulted in this duty and simply sent her home, she was disgraced and would look forward to a life of being an unmarriageable old maid serving as a lowly servant to the rest of her father's clan. Being returned like damaged goods after marriage was a serious stigma.

Displaying a strength of will and a keen intelligence, she seduced Judah by masquerading as a harlot. She then procured from him his undeniable possessions – his seal and staff as a pledge for Judah's payment to her for her services. When she later appeared at his tent pregnant with his child (twins as it turns out) and could produce his seal and staff, she had not only outwitted him, but shamed him for shirking his obligations to her in the past and secured a future for herself and her progeny in his tents. In 30 verses in Genesis 38, the writer has condensed a story of ambiguity, meaning, character development and turgidity worthy of high literary regard. It is not, by accident then, that Tamar is a progenitor of the line of David through one of her twins, Perez.

Mary MAGDALENE

RICHARD MALMED

Mary Magdalene is undeniably one of the most intriguing characters in the New Testament. Unfortunately, for the past 1,500 years until recently, she has been all too conveniently dismissed as a prostitute. Pope Gregory I in the fifth century through a misreading of two consecutive passages in Luke 7:36-50 and Luke 8 and John 11:12 declared her a prostitute and, thus, disabused any Christian that she had some intellectual or spiritual influence on Jesus, and could serve as a disciple or preacher.

In doing so, he and the Catholic Church with its copartners in government, the feudal monarchs, were able to deny females access to all roles in government, power, family functions, inheritance and virtually all other aspects of importance in society.

In effect, the Popes and the subsequent leaders of the Catholic Church and the feudal monarchs gave the populace two female role models – Mary, Jesus' mother and Mary Magdalene. These two myths were tremendously instrumental in substantiating male power politically and within marriage for the past many centuries. A true analysis of the historical Mary Magdalene however would have produced a far different result.

There is also a Mary referred to as living in Bethany. The Gospel of John identifies her as the same woman who washed Jesus' feet with her hair and anointed them with oil. According to John, this took place in Bethany. In Luke 7, it was a fictional event which was used in a parable to contrast those who showed the most devotion and were entitled to the most forgiveness. Luke then proceeds in Chapter 8 to number Mary among those traveling with the Apostles. Other than a comment in John, there is no basis for connecting the fictional prostitute in Luke with Mary. Yet the male dominated church conflated the two images to define Mary as a reprehensible prostitute, who was essentially a lowly creature although forgiven as a result of her repentance.

It is interesting however that this Mary who appears in John as anointing Jesus in Bethany is also the sister or cousin of Lazarus. This Lazarus is the same young man whom Jesus is credited with raising from the dead. This particular miracle suggests a number of important facts which tantalizingly reveal a number of interesting connections. Once again, it is John alone who is the source of the story. In John, the sisters Mary and Martha send word to Jesus that Lazarus is sick, but although Jesus is said to hold great affection for Lazarus and his relatives Mary and Martha, he dismissed their request for haste and delayed for several days before coming to Bethany. After a delay of two days, Jesus and his followers take the lengthy journey to Bethany. Jesus had been in the upper

Galilea, yet Bethany is several days journey to the south in Judea, about two miles from Jerusalem.

On his arrival after abruptly comforting Mary and Martha who have reproached him for not coming sooner, he turns to Lazarus in a burial cave. What happens next is an eerie foreshadowing of the events during Jesus' crucifixion. Jesus is taken to the family tomb and asks that the stone covering the entrance be rolled back. Without any further ceremony or prayer, Jesus commands Lazarus to come out of the tomb. Lazarus miraculously complies.

The writer of the John Gospel may have either unwittingly or purposely disclosed the beginnings of a conspiracy to free Jesus from the subsequent death by crucifixion. The period of Lazarus apparent "death" is commensurate with Jesus' eventual apparent death. Lazarus and Mary Magdalene (whom John identifies as the anointing Mary Magdalene) are close associates of Jesus. It is possible that in John, he reveals that this was a dress rehearsal for Jesus' fake death. Just as in Romeo and Juliet, it had been known for many centuries, particularly in the Middle East, that certain drugs would create the appearance of a deathlike coma. Mandrake or as the gospels called it, "gall" could have been administered to Jesus while he was on the cross. At some point in Mark, Jesus is offered wine mixed with myrrh which he refused Mark 15:13. Then a mere six hours later, Jesus says the famous "My God, my God, why has thou forsaken me?" Mark 15:34. At that point he is given a spongeful of what is claimed to be vinegar, after which he promptly dies. Joseph of Arimathea then claimed the body from Pilate and had it taken to his family tomb where a stone was rolled across the door of the sepulcher.

Since Mary Magdalene is present at Lazarus' rising from the dead, Jesus' crucifixion and at his tomb when the body is discovered missing, it is obvious that Mary Magdalene was an important character in Jesus' life and probably his wife. Her act in dressing the body of Jesus is the work of a man's wife. She is the first to discover the open tomb and report the missing body. In the gospels themselves then, she must be accorded very high esteem in any religion based on Jesus' life.

In the Gospel of Mary, a gnostic gospel which was excluded from the Catholic canon, Mary is considered to be the highest ranking of the disciples who had Jesus' ear and is specially tutored by him in the mysteries of his faith. She is also an obvious love object of Jesus.

Yet she has been condemned as a prostitute for the ages. Another line of inquiry attempts to define just who Mary Magdalene really was? There certainly was a town of Magdala near Capernaum in the northern Galilee where Jesus' ministry began. Second names for people at the time were rare and even then were either a patronymic used to designate that they were someone's son (bar or ibn) or had an unusual occupation, but women in general rarely were so designated. Since Magdala was a small town, it would have been possible that giving her the sobriquet – Magdalene – may have clearly identified her among the many Marys. It would also have been possible that her family had substantial land holdings in the town and had acquired the second name as a medieval lord might have by adding the family fiefdom as his last name.

In any case, if she had not only become a follower of Jesus but one respected by Jesus, and the other Apostles, she must have acquired an education so that she could hold her own as a woman with Jesus and the Apostles. For a woman to acquire an education would have been rare unless she came from a family of some degree of wealth. This might suggest that she was monied and of a higher socio-economic class.

The Gospel of Mary says that the other Apostles were jealous because Jesus "kissed Mary on the mouth." Others refer to her as the "most beloved" Apostle. The most impressive reference to her occurs in the Gospel of Mary where she claims to have had special knowledge given to her by Jesus and is held in high esteem by the other Apostles. In fact she knows Peter's antipathy because he contests her claims but is quickly silenced by Levi.

The da Vinci Code famously and convincingly claims that she was Jesus' wife, bore his child and escaped to Southern France where her child became the progenitor of a dynasty and was in fact the Holy Grail. (sang real = san greal, Royal Blood =Holy Grail). He also makes a convincing argument that Mary attended the Last Supper and sat next to Jesus in the center of the painting and was in fact "the most beloved disciple." Such an assertion would imply that Leonardo da Vinci was part of a secret society which venerated Mary. A number of his other paintings by their curious ambiguities give other hints to da Vinci's esoteric images of Mary and Jesus.

Mary Magdalene can then be seen as fulfilling her role as an "eshektal" as described in Proverbs 31. She is his helpmate, right hand man and general confidante. If women in Christian communities had been allowed to assume such roles, we would have more than the heroic women scattered over the pages of history than we do now. Certainly, Catherine the Great of Russia, Elizabeth I of England, Jean D'Arc of France and very few others managed to shoulder their way into historical prominence. Outside of the saints, the Christian community has few others. It seems then that the Christian myths of the two Marys have kept women, in effect, cloistered and bescarved in a Middle Eastern tradition. Certainly, these myths have been dangerous.

Judas

RICHARD MALMED

Judas is the most problematic figure in the gospels. The first and often most important issue is his name "Iscariot." The majority of scholars agree that this means he was a member of the Sicarii – a revolutionary group who preyed on Jews who supported the Roman occupation and the Roman occupiers. The name comes from a sharp pointed dagger, a sicar, easily concealed in their loose garments. It must then be conceded that Judah was a passionate, anti-Roman revolutionary.

While popular culture depicts the other disciples as illiterate Galilean peasants who spent their time in Jesus entourage praying and healing. In reality, they were nothing of the sort. Nor did Jesus expect them to be anything less than warriors. Jesus clearly states in Matthew 10.34, "Think not I come to send peace on earth. I come not to send peace, but a sword." The disciples were also armed as Jesus ordered. "He that hath no sword, let him sell his garment and buy one." Luke 22:36.

Another disciple was known as Simon Zelotes (i.e. the zealot – a secret group dedicated to guerilla war against the Romans.)

Disciples James and John were known as Boanerges or Sons of Thunder, Mark 3:17. Included among the many interpretations of the meaning of this designation is a form of nom de guerre.

When the Romans and Temple priests came to arrest Jesus in the Garden of Gethsemane, one of the disciples drew a sword and sliced someone's (possibly a member of the Temple guard) ear off.

In short, these disciples appear to be battle hardened veterans of guerilla warfare in Galilee. But Judas was different, he was not from the rough and tumble lands of Galilee; he was a Judean. For the most part, he would have been educated and more sophisticated. The fact that he was designated the treasurer of the group suggests the faith that Jesus and the disciples had in him. It would have been his job to collect donations and buy provisions for the wandering troop. More importantly, he would have had a completely different and easily recognizable accent from the Galileans. His Judean tones would stand out to any observer. Judeans were considered to be urban, educated and sophisticated compared to the Galileans who might be considered country bumpkins.

One liability that Judas brought with him was that he had been in an earlier uprising against the Romans along with Simon Zelotes and Thaddeus. Undoubtedly, Roman security had been questioning all of its available resources to identify and locate the perpetrators of the rebellion.

As any totalitarian force, it had many methods at its command to gather information. It certainly had spies. In fact, Paul had been one prior to his conversion to the Jesus movement. Certainly, Rome had money. It had many criminal arrestees who could be persuaded to give up any information. Judas probably had become a security risk for Jesus.

It is difficult to determine exactly what Jesus' true agenda would have been. Despite the presence of several armed warriors in his group of disciples, Jesus does not appear to have had a warlike agenda. He certainly was not a warrior or a wartime commander himself; his only background was probably as an apprentice carpenter and an itinerant scholar. His early ministry began with John the Baptist – another nonviolent minister. His parables and sermons deal mainly with meekness, piety, atonement and devotion to God. Hardly, the dossier for a revolutionary war-time leader such as the Maccabees family of the previous Jewish Dynasty – the Hasmoneans. It is more likely that these armed men in his entourage functioned only as body guards in the lawless lands of the Galilee during his ministry.

Moreover, any educated observer would have to know that Judea was not ripe for any kind of military conflict. As usual, the Jewish nation was split into many different blocs whom it would be difficult to unite. Obviously, the Sadducees were beholden to the Romans for their priestly status from which they derived a very nice living. There were many publicans – tax collectors – who did very well as tax collecting agents of Rome. The landlords and the middle class such as it was were able to put up with some Roman indignities for a comfortable lifestyle. The Pharisees are a more difficult group to analyze. The Essenes documents, the Dead Sea Scrolls, revile the Pharisees as "lovers of smooth things." They are depicted as being more interested in extremely detailed observance of empty rituals to the detriment of true spirit of the Torah. Jesus on frequent occasions pointed out the hypocrisy or overzealousness of the Pharisees and often states the law was made for man, not man for the law. In short, the Jews were a divided fractious bunch who could not be expected to conduct an organized military campaign against such an overwhelming, disciplined, trained, battle hardened foe as the legions of the Roman Empire. Although an occasional guerilla skirmish, or an attack on an isolated party of soldiers was possible, a large scale military attack was unthinkable – certainly to Jesus.

As always when dealing in matters relating to the history of Jesus, it is important to note that most if not all of the source material comes from the New Testament. It is also well recognized among scholars that this material was written down from 20 to 90 years or more after the crucifixion by writers who were not eyewitnesses to the events. Judas is mentioned about 50 years after the crucifixion in Mark 3:19. Before that there was a compilation of documents attributed to Paul, known as Acts which were written between 50 CE and 64 CE. Matthew and Luke written about 20 years after Mark, draw heavily on Mark as well as a source common to both of them known by scholars as the Q Source. Paul or Paul's scribe simply refer to an unidentified attributable incident, when he says "that the Lord Jesus Christ, on the night he was betrayed, took bread and when he had given thanks, he broke it and said…" That is the only Pauline reference mentioned of betrayal and does not refer to Judas. The word actually used for "betrayed," however actually means "handed over." Later translations familiar with the later gospels used the word betrayed to conform to those gospels. In Acts, Judas – not having died – is depicted as still with the 11 disciples long after the crucifixion.

When Matthew wrote his account in about 82 – 85 CE, there were only 11 disciples. Matt. 28:16-20. Other verses however refer to all 12 disciples including Judas. Matt. 19:28, Luke 22:28-30.

In about 67 to 70 CE, the Romans completely destroyed the Jewish Temple, leveled Jerusalem and scattered the Jews. By this time, the Pauline version of the Jesus Movement had gained roots in Asia Minor and his followers were anxious to distance themselves from the traditional Jewish religion. Only at that time, the references to Judas' alleged betrayal are found in the gospels.

Neither of the insertions has much credibility. First, they were written over 50 years later and not by eyewitnesses. But the stories hold little water. In the one story, Judas is alleged to have sold Jesus out for 30 pieces of silver. Since Judas was the treasurer of the group and by tradition had been trained as a Judean merchant, it seems unlikely that he would have accepted such a low sum as his primary motivation. If he were interested in money and did not mind doing something reprehensible, he could simply have made off with the treasury. In another story, Judas' change of heart is attributable to "Satan having entered him." The satanic element has no basis in Jewish literature. For Jews, there was no Satan because all men were responsible for their own acts and could not blame an outside agency for the evil that they themselves may have done. This Satan reference comes from a dualist literary tradition in Asia Minor – probably Zoroastrian or Gnosticism, but it was clearly not a Jewish concept.

All the foregoing, notwithstanding, we still do not know what was motivating Jesus, and what Judas.

As to Jesus, we know that in Jerusalem, he committed himself to three separate actions which might define his motives.

First, he entered the City of Jerusalem riding on a donkey in the precise manner that fulfilled a prophecy of Zechariah. Jesus had carefully arranged for the donkey and a colt and the other accoutrements in fulfillment of the prophecy. To those who knew their Bible, Jesus was calling himself the Messiah. He had done something similar on the first official act of his ministry when he addressed the congregation during Sabbath services in his hometown of Nazareth. Luke 4 (16-30) While, undoubtedly, his followers were able to stir up enthusiasm among the pilgrims, it is uncertain whether this even was a resounding success when introduced for the first time in Jerusalem.

Second, he overturned the tables of the money changers in the Temple courtyard. If that didn't attract attention, nothing would. It was done directly under the noses of the Roman guards who would see directly down into the Temple courtyard from the higher walls of the Antonia Palace and observe everything that went on. To the Romans, it was a major disturbance of the peace. To the Temple authorities, the Sadducees, it was a major insult. The Sadducees controlled the Jewish religion by requiring all sacrifices to be made at the Temple in Jerusalem. The pilgrims could not be expected to transport the "perfect" animals required so they were required to buy them in the Temple courtyard. But the pilgrims could not use coins with the human impressions on their face in the transaction since that would be an act of idolatry within the Temple precincts. So these humble often unsophisticated peasants were required to exchange the coins at ruinous exchange rates. The Sadducees profited handsomely from all of this, and for the past 500 years were able to maintain a hereditary, dynastic control over the Jerusalem Temple. Jesus was calling all of this into question: the very institution of sacrifice, the commerce on Temple grounds, the hereditary position of the Sadducees, and not so indirectly, the Sadducees favorable status with the Romans. Jesus certainly was directing his attack on the money changers against the sacrifice tradition, which had persisted in Judaism and against the Sadducees who controlled that institution. But not the Romans.

Similarly, Jesus appears to have had a number of doctrinal disputes with the Pharisees who insisted in strict observance of prescribed rituals. It was however a long standing Jewish tradition to question and dispute authorities – the Talmud is full of such honorable disputes.

Jesus, also, never chose a ascetic, monastic lifestyle similar to the Essenes.

It is hard to categorize Jesus or determine what his motivation was. It has been suggested that he was an "apocalypticist" or one who believed that God would intervene in human affairs, subject the wicked to punishment and the righteous – even if poor and meek – to just rewards. It has been suggested that he believed that the divine intervention was imminent and that people should repent very soon to prepare themselves for the coming of the Lord.

Given these interpretations, it is difficult to see what motivation Judas would have had for a betrayal. His status, however, as a security risk for Jesus both as a Sicarii revolutionary and as a Judean, may have suggested to the Romans that Jesus was harboring subversive elements and had to be a revolutionary. It is suggested that Judas' betrayal may have been an inadvertent one. To the Sadducees, Jesus' participation in the money changer incident would have been well known. Jesus' daily presence in the city was also well known and his nightly location easily discovered.

The evil, however, in believing Judas was a betrayer is that it created centuries of anti-Semitic feeling. Judas' name alone implies that he was a Jew. The revilement of the Jews in the early church and its gospels and letters was a direct attempt to distance the Christian movement, largely in Asia Minor, among the pagan converts from the Jews of Jerusalem who had been defeated and slaughtered by the Romans from 67 – 70 CE, before most of the gospels were written. Judas became a convenient figure to rest this anti-Jewish sentiment on, and he remained so for centuries later in much of Christian literature. That he intentionally harmed Jesus cannot be supported by any reasonable review of the facts.

Constantine

RICHARD MALMED

Constantine had many major influences on Christianity; some extremely favorable, some particularly harmful. While he elevated Christianity from a much persecuted, frequently underground sect to the designated religion of the Roman Empire in 325 CE he introduced unfortunate concepts into the doctrine which have been pernicious to this day.

Constantine's influence on history and on Christianity is inexplicable in rational terms. He was born the son of a well-regarded military man in the upper echelons of the military hierarchy. Constantius, his father, had taken a concubine, Helena, who gave birth to Constantine in about 275 CE. Previously, Helena had been a stable maid and was subsequently relegated to a minor role in Constantius' household when he married Theodora, the step daughter of the emperor. Constantius, however continued to recognize Constantine as his son and helped him advance through the military ranks as his protégé. Constantine, throughout his life, continued to have a close relationship with his mother. As frequently occurred in Roman history, succession to leadership was accomplished by murder, assassinations, treachery and civil war. Constantine pursued each of these after the death of his father when Constantine found himself among the final four men contesting for the seat of emperor.

While first winning a number of battles in the civil war which ensued, Constantine was engaged in what was to be a decisive battle against Maxentius, one major rival, at what is known as the Milvian Bridge.

This particular battle and the previous military engagements were fought for no other reason than to advance the personal ambitions of either two of the four men. There was no spiritual, economic, ethnic or other motivation behind each of the bloody and ruinous conflicts. Each of the men did not champion any particular political, ethnic, financial or religious movement. Various rumors however have it that Constantine had a vision or dream that, if he had his soldiers adorn their shields with an emblem associated with Jesus Christ he would win the battle. The symbol was a combination of the Greek letters chi and rho which were part of the word Christos meaning anointed. It was not the cross, as many believe. Constantine won this battle decisively as he had won the other previous ones by his own superior military discipline and tactics. No unusual intervention in the battle appears to have occurred. In his later ascension to the throne, he resorted to murder, poison and marriage to a rival's daughter as the means to power rather than assistance from any religious force.

At the time and throughout his life, Constantine was not a Christian convert until immediately prior to his death. But he had been known prior to the battle and subsequently, as one who did not favor persecution of the Christians. He was not the first to advocate this tolerance of Christians, as part of a political tactic.

It is also difficult to understand why Constantine would pursue the political course of declaring Christianity the religion of the Roman Empire. The path to political power in the Roman Empire since Caesar had been to court the support of the Roman soldiers first. Many of these men followed a form of paganism known as Mithraism, and Constantine was believed to have been a follower as well. Considering that it was such a widely held belief in the early 300s CE, and was frequently espoused by the military, Mithraism had the potential to be a strong influence in the world. A prominent historian, Ernest Renan in 1882, said that, if the growth of Christianity had not occurred, the world would have been Mithraic. The two religions were extremely different. In fact, the only similarity between the two appears to be that of the birthday of their central figure. Mithras was supposedly born on December 25. Jesus' birthday was not deemed to be December 25 until sometime much later. In fact, the previous religious figure of Sol Invictus (the epitome of the Sun God) predated both. His cult claimed December 25 as his birthday. It is generally calculated that Jesus was actually born in the spring. It is also more probable that December 25 was chosen as the birthdate of Mithra and Jesus to coincide with the popular holiday on December 25 to accommodate the local population's feasts already celebrated on that day, which was close to the winter solstice.

What little is known of Mithraism comes from pictures of Mithra killing a bull and being drenched with its blood. It is believed that in their initiation rites, men were also marked with bull's blood in this fashion. Mithra was the god of war, and possessed great masculine strength. Membership in the cult was limited to men and its rites were a closely guarded secret, but it seems to have encouraged soldiers and military leaders to be ruthless in battle and show no mercy to those weaker than themselves.

Nonetheless, Mithraism had a swift decline in popularity at the same time as Christianity rose, this was due to the almost single-handed efforts of Constantine who elevated Christianity over all other cults at the time.

The next political element was the common Roman citizenry. Christians had grown to a sizable percentage of the population, but nowhere enough to be considered a substantial political force. Estimates are about 25 percent. Traditional Jews also were well represented among the population. The Christians were not particularly wealthy and held little power since they were usually in the lower socio-economic classes. Pursuing favor with them gave Constantine little in the way of political or financial power.

Many of the pagan religions had much in common with each other. Frequently, the people were members of more than one god's temple. The gods, originally, had come from aspects of nature – the sun, the moon, the earth, the sea or animals such as the bull, were worshipped for fertility or agricultural prosperity. Mithraism seemed to worship the bull. Later, more complex abstract elements were worshipped such as truth, wisdom or beauty. These gods had little to do with advancing a moral code and usually indulged themselves in rape, sexual exploits, treachery, thievery, lechery and drunkenness against their fellow gods and humans. Their temples were the centerpieces of most urban environments and deeply rooted in local festivals. It was not difficult for people of one pagan religion to switch to the similar gods of their conquerors since their gods' attributes were similar. Worship consisted mainly of bringing animals to the temple for sacrifice and asking the gods so honored for personal prosperity in farming, hunting or war. Often, their rites included sex with temple prostitutes. Concepts such as piety, chastity, charity, atonement were largely absent from any pagan moral code.

The Christian religion was different in so many ways that it generated many conflicts with the pagans. As a monotheistic religion, it demanded an exclusive devotion to one God, who had little to do with nature, its cycles, or its fertility. It insisted upon a moral code and promised severe eternal punishment for noncompliance. Personal sacrifice, piety, care for the poor or weak were central to the religion. In the words of Jesus, it preached nonviolence and atonement for sins, among other doctrines. Its rewards were not earthly prosperity or fleshly delights; but salvation in an eternal afterlife. Its main appeal was to the poor and weak to whom the benefits of this world might be denied, but afforded in the next. At that time, it was believed that only royalty or nobility entitled people to an afterlife. Christianity promised it to all who would follow its precepts. It also required belief in a number of abstract principles, rather than objective real world physical realities. In short, it was markedly different from the belief system of the ordinary Roman citizen.

There was, in short, little of political benefit to be gained by Constantine's eventual espousal of the Christian religion as the national religion of the Roman Empire. The political or economic force it drew were from the poor and the weak. It was not a favorite of his primary political base – the military or the aristocracy. It made him no friends among the pagan clergy.

It seems that Constantine's designation of Christianity as the national religion was attributable only to a desire to please his mother, Helena. She was born of extremely poor, common stock and in histories of the time she was identified as a stable maid. Perhaps she identified with the lower socio-economic classes who had converted or she identified, as the cast aside concubine of a Roman general, with the lowly and disenfranchised. In any case, when her son rose to power and claimed the seal as uncontested Emperor of the Roman Empire, she used him to advance the status of Christianity. Her son raised her to the rank of Augusta, brought her to his ruling seat to serve in his court. After his accession to power, Constantine gave her liberal access to his treasury to take trips to Jerusalem and build a number of churches there and elsewhere.

On the other hand, Constantine had little attachment to his own wife or son, Crispus, both of whom he later murdered, apparently in retaliation for a plot against him.

After establishing Christianity as the religion of the Roman Empire, Constantine commanded the recognized leaders of the Christian church to assemble at Nicaea in 325 CE to formalize a standard doctrine to govern the whole church, which in turn, would control religion throughout the Empire. This assembly would insert many questionable influences into the religion and the western world. This combination of church and state created an oppressive power for over 1,600 years.

Perhaps the first influence was that Constantine as the secular head of state acquired control of the religion and its leader. The first pope under Constantine, Sylvester I, was securely under Constantine's control and deeply beholden to him for advancing Christianity in such a cataclysmic way. For many generations thereafter, the church became an enforcement arm of the state for rulers for at least 1,600 years by creating the doctrine of the divine right of kings. The church was thus to serve the political ambitions of monarchs and support their dynasties, quell their rebellions, enslave their populations in feudal serfdom, and obstruct reform and the dissemination of alternative thought as well as new ideas and innovation.

The controlling doctrine of Christianity of turning the other cheek, the veneration of the poor and meek, the practices of personal sacrifice, and abstinence, martyrdom become powerful tools in quelling insurrections by the feudal serfs. They often became docile and subservient rather than risk excommunication or disapprobation by the village priest. Among the more perverted practices was "droit du seigneur." The right of the ruling local vassal to take the virginity of females in his domain before their husbands on their wedding nights. They enabled a class of aristocrats to pursue a life of combat, hunting or courtly luxury while the vast majority of the churches' believers were held in abject feudal servitude as farm laborers. In short, the church had been enlisted to continue the brutal policies of the Roman Empire, or feudal overlords.

Part of the manner in which the serfs were controlled were a series of oppressive doctrines. One of which held God was not approachable directly, but only through a church representative. The term vicar implies that religious communication can only be effective through a vicarious experience. This concept inserted the church as a necessary intermediary in the process of prayer. This contravened one of Jesus' main themes in his conflict with the Sadducees who insisted on controlling the rite of sacrifice at the Temple in Jerusalem. All church works were in Latin – an obscure language for the serfs. Since the reading of the Bible was forbidden to the serfs and permitted only to a limited number of scholars, only the priests could interpret the scriptures.

Another doctrine was that of Sola Fide, or as translated "only faith." This tenet asserted that belief or the total acceptance of all church doctrine was more important than either charity or good works or atonement for sins. By substituting total devotion to a church hierarchy and its dogma for a moral code or personal salvation, the church compelled the largely uneducated serf not to seek individual growth or achievement. By the giving or withholding of access to the church rites – communion, baptism, last rights, confession, etc., many of which occurred in full public view, the peasants were condemned to isolation for failure to adhere to the church. Deviation from the precise elements of faith as dictated by the church would lead to excommunication. Isolation from the community meant madness or death.

Eventually, the concept of the "Divine Right of Kings" supported the monarch and the Church. The king held his office as an agent of God and, in effect, anyone who interfered with his edicts or sought to rebel was defying God, and subject to excommunication.

Helena may have been Christianity's greatest proponent if she is the one who influenced Constantine to raise it to the status of official state religion. She certainly was extremely devout and, after Constantine's rise to emperor, founded many churches in Jerusalem and Europe.

She, however, is best known as a collector of relics from the Holy Land. During a trip to Palestine in about 326 – 328 CE, she had two churches built – one in Bethlehem – at the purported site of Jesus' nativity, and on the Mount of Olives – the site of Jesus' purported ascension. Neither site is today believed to be historically accurate. She also is identified as the builder of the Saint Catherine's Monastery on Mt. Sinai in Egypt at the purported site of the Burning Bush in about 330 CE. This also is not believed to be historically accurate. Her information came from dubious sources some 300 years after the actual events took place.

Although accounts differ, she visited the site of a temple to Venus constructed by Hadrian after the complete destruction of Jerusalem. Tradition holds that she tore down this temple to erect a Christian church. During the excavation, she discovered three crosses which she was told, were from Jesus' crucifixion. Helena insisted upon a test of the crosses to determine their authenticity. Pieces of each cross were touched to the woman afflicted by a fatal disease. The first two crosses had no effect on her condition, but from the third, she was miraculously cured. From this, Helena deduced the third was the true cross. At this site, she erected the Church of the Holy Sepulcher. Again, this site is not believed to be historically accurate.

Helena returned to Rome in about 327 bringing large parts of this cross which remain today in her private chapel, and is now known as the Basilica of the Holy Cross in Jerusalem, maintained by the Cistercian monks. Because of the many relics from early Christianity she brought back from her trip, she may have started the relic tradition in which churches throughout Europe claimed to have some physical object to be venerated and sought by pilgrims. This form of idolatry persisted for 1,200 years.

In addition to the cross, Helena, it is claimed, brought back Jesus' tunic and sent it to Trier as well as pieces of the rope with which Jesus was tied to the cross.

These relics were successful in drawing numerous pilgrims to churches in which the relics were placed. From that point forward, the claim of relics expanded exponentially to include body parts of numerous saints, or figures in Biblical history. John the Baptist's parts are perhaps the most prolific. The relics and the pilgrimages they drew were not only points of great pride, but sources of much income for the churches and towns in which they were situated. With the worship of many of their religious figures physical parts, many saints became the object of worship and their alleged attributes sought by veneration and the burning of candles in much the same way as pagan gods and their idols had been worshipped before.

In addition, the relics and icons of the many venerated human saints or monks, began to become the subject of worship and drew pilgrimages as well. Over the next 400 years, the church fathers debated the propriety of this form of worship in a series of ecumenical counsels, but the practice being quite lucrative persisted.

Eventually in 754 CE, the relics and icons were banned by the church fathers as forms of idolatry. Thirty-three years later however in what was called the "Second Council of Nicaea," a wider circle of clerics met and reinstituted the veneration of relics and the icons of saints and monks. It thus became Church doctrine that parishioners, and especially pilgrims, were encouraged to worship physical objects and images of venerated church notables. In this way, the church had reinstated a form of idolatry. Many contended that this practice violated the First Commandment and further encouraged elevation of certain humans to divine status.

In subtle ways, idolatry of this sort reinstates many of the flaws or heresies of the pagan religions. By worshipping multiple images, monotheism was no longer a principle tenet of western religion. Although the Church had previously split the God head into the trinity by adding to a father image, the image of a young virile son as well as the Holy Spirit. It had by this time made Mary, Jesus' mother, a symbol of passive female chastity and object of separate worship. By adding relics, saints and monks to the mix and giving them separate attributes, parishioners were encouraged to go to various of the physical symbols which met their individual needs – fertility, health, wealth, and even for specific afflictions or benefits. Separate chapels were incorporated in the churches to accommodate separate worship of these icons. Viewed in a larger historical context, the Church had returned to a time before Abraham when multiple gods and physical objects were worshipped.

Monotheism does not merely limit man to the worship of one God. It also includes the concept of avoiding anthropomorphism. In short, God is not a physical essence like man, but a spirit far superior to man whose acts are unknowable because he dealt in a larger context than man could imagine.

The pagan form of worship of a physical object to ask for personal benefits – wealth, fertility, etc. was clearly contrary to including a moral code in religion. Concepts such as charity, atonement, responsibility to the community, fair commercial dealings, accommodation of the spiritual world with the physical as well as other abstract ideas had advanced the western world on a higher trajectory. By returning to idolatry, the Christian Church was regressing. Therefore, Helena, although having the best of intentions, had imported an infectious idea into the Christianity of Constantine. Helena and Constantine set Christianity on a course incorporating many concepts which impeded progress until the Renaissance.

Constantine further imported the hierarchical structure of the Roman Army into the Church organization. And he thereby standardized and froze Christianity's theology into an orthodox belief, and developed a mechanism whereby the king was supported by the Church in an oppressive feudal system which existed for over a thousand years known as the Dark Ages. He created a partnership of church and state which helped suppress any thoughts of rebellion by the serfs – the concept of divine right of kinds, confession, excommunication were all used to gain a firm control over the peasant population. By the introduction of relics into the religion along with the multiplication of divine objects of worship in the saints and their symbols or relics defeated the principles of monotheism, and individual responsibility for moral acts, piety, atonement when a lit candle to a specific saint might suffice.

THREE
Kings

RICHARD MALMED

The story of the Three Kings is told only in the Gospel according to Matthew. In brief, the Three Kings hear of the birth of "the King of the Jews" and follow a star traveling from West to East and bearing gifts of gold, frankincense and myrrh. Herod, then the king appointed by the Romans, heard of this and asked these men to come to him and explain their visit. When he discovered that they had come to pay homage to a newly born child who was to fulfill a biblical prophecy that the child would be born in Bethlehem of the House of David and become "King of the Jews." He asked of the men where "Christ" shall be born and they replied in Bethlehem. Herod then urged them to seek Jesus out and report back to him so that he too might worship him. The Wise Men departed and followed the star which stopped its transit over the young child. They then worshipped the child, gave him gifts of gold, frankincense and myrrh. Then warned in a dream by God that they should not return to Herod, they returned home. Joseph also warned in a dream to avoid Herod, left with Mary and Jesus for Egypt and did not return until Herod's death. In the meantime, Herod fearful of a rival to his throne, murdered all children under the age of two in Bethlehem, the so-called "murder of innocents." No other historical source accepts this murder of children as historical fact.

It is suggested that the theme of the "murder of innocents" is totally apocryphal. It appears to have been inserted into the gospel to suggest that there was some connection between Jesus and Moses. Moses of course as did Jesus, survived the King's mandate to murder first-born children. There are other themes in the gospel which liken Jesus to Moses. It must been seen as a literary device rather than a historical fact. No other historical record supports the notion that this mass murder occurred.

The Gospel of Matthew is believed to have been written between 70 and 90 CE – about 40 years at least after Jesus' crucifixion. Matthew is generally believed to have been an educated man writing in a polished Greek style. This gospel otherwise draws heavily on that of Mark, believed to have been written about 20 years earlier. It adopts directly much of Mark's text (600 of 661 of Mark's verses). Some 220 verses appear in both Luke and Matthew, but there are many that are unique to Matthew alone.

Dating the gospel at this time, places it squarely after the destruction of the Temple by the Romans in the war between 66 and 73 CE. By this time, Christianity had become a separate religion created mostly out of Paul's ministry to the pagans of Asia Minor and Greece.

The gospel began by tracing Jesus' ancestry from Abraham to his father Joseph, while in the succeeding verses, the writer of Matthew attributed a virgin birth to Mary of Jesus by the Holy Spirit. Matthew saw Jesus as the new Moses and attempted to reconcile Judaism with the new Christianity. A crucial factor in Matthew's time was the issue of whether Jesus was to be seen as divine. While Mark does not support such claims, Matthew and his contemporary Luke do. Scholars for the most part conclude that both Matthew and Luke are both derivative of a prior narrative for the "Q source," whose date of authorship is unclear. Nonetheless, because of other elements in the gospels, both Matthew and Luke must be dated after the destruction of the Temple.

There are a number of elements in the three Wise Men story which have been incorporated into the Christmas myth. It is difficult to reconcile how Jesus could be descended from David in order to claim the title "King of the Jews" as his hereditary birthright when his lineage is traced through Joseph, while Mary was to have been impregnated by the Holy Spirit. Mark the gospel written a generation prior in time, has no reference to a virgin birth, nor a line of descent from David.

Similarly, Matthew solves the problem of the David prophecy by noting that Jesus was born in Bethlehem. Mark makes no mention of his place of birth.

Then the Three Wise Men came to worship Jesus. While it is traditional to have these men be designated as "kings," the gospel simply calls them wise men or magi. This term probably identifies them as Persian priests or sorcerers. Tradition has it that there were three, but in fact, no number is given.

The story clearly describes them as coming from the East, and following a star to discover what they refer to as "The King of the Jews." The star is described as "standing still" over Bethlehem so that these wise men may find it. These descriptions require the conclusion that the wise men are following an astrological calculation and must therefore be "magi" – or Zoroastrian sorcerers.

The story creates many difficult factual issues. Throughout Jesus' ministry, he is described as having been born in Nazareth in Galilee, yet, the biblical prophecy linking him to King David requires that he be born in Bethlehem (in Judea). Matthew clearly put him directly in Bethlehem for his birth, but had him escape Herod's "Murder of the innocents" by fleeing to Egypt and returning to Galilee and Nazareth. There is no explanation as to how his Galilean parents came to live in Bethlehem several difficult day's journey away, and in and entirely different country at the time.

Luke also puts Jesus' genealogy through his father Joseph to the Davidian house but repeats the virgin birth of Jesus through Mary by the Holy Spirit. He had Jesus born in Nazareth, however but travel to Bethlehem to comply with a census decree requiring the Jews to engage in an improbably massive series of migrations to return to their home towns where they may be counted and appropriately taxed. Again, Galilee and Judea were entirely separate countries at this time.

Nonetheless, Jesus' birth according to two gospels occurs in Bethlehem. Despite the incalculable number of astrologers in the world between then and the present, no such star, constellation, meteor or any other heavenly body has been identified to follow the path of the star of the Wise Men in Matthew. No astrological reading has been shown to have predicted the birth of a figure such as Jesus during the range of years attributed to his birth. Despite the incredible brutality of a story in which the entire city of Bethlehem's male children under the age of two are slain at Herod's command, there is no historical or astrological record of any such event.

The gifts of the Wise Men are difficult factual issues as well. If three men, whether kings, magi or other designation but obvious foreigners came to a town the size of Bethlehem (or even Nazareth) and gave expensive and unusual gifts to the son of poor parents, it would have been the talk of the town forever. Jesus from that point in the narrative is not heard from again until about thirty years later when he joined John the Baptist's ministry. Neither Mark, nor Luke include this noteworthy event in their gospels.

The gifts themselves are interesting by themselves. Gold an obvious gift to one who may be king, but myrrh is a symbol of death. It was an oil used in embalming dead bodies. Why anyone would give such a gift to a recently born child in real life is a mystery. It might even be deemed to be a curse, similar to the wicked witch in "Sleeping Beauty." It obviously is a literary device used to foreshadow a significant event of death in the future. Frankincense is a strange gift to a poor family of peasants who would have little use for it; however, it did have substantial commercial value.

Jews in the first century would have rejected out of hand a narrative relying on astrology and the influence of Persian or Zoroastrian magi on their king or messiah. Jesus throughout his gospel depictions shows himself to be an educated, devout Jew. He even searched for ways in which to be more devout and never tried to import Greek, Zoroastrian, Canaanite or pagan concepts into the religion. Jesus, if he were to be a messiah, would have been one for the Jewish community at the time, not the Persian.

To first century Jews, the idea of astrology was not at all compatible with Jewish thought. Essentially, astrology is a study of the stars and constellations in relation to the earth. As such, it makes earth the center of the universe – a concept rejected by learned Egyptians who saw the sun as the center of the universe. The Jews, unlike most pagan religions, did not rely on observations of the celestial bodies to determine or predict events. Of course in agrarian societies, sun and moon cycles were very important and held to be manifestations of God if not God itself. The Jews had long previously rejected the notion of praying to the sun, moon, natural elements such as rain, the sea, the winds or animals. When Jews became monotheistic, they chose to believe in an abstract, spiritual God, who by his acts, encouraged belief in a highly developed code of ethical and moral behavior. And this code promised, in some unknown and unknowable way, divine reward or retribution for human acts. To determine the course of human events by studying the stars, and discovering personal aspects by identifying oneself with some supposed attribute of a star, planet or constellation, whose attributes had been assigned and identified by magi was anathema. It suggested a predestination or fatalism – a concept never accepted in Judaism. Yet, the reliance on astrology by this story was incorporated into Pauline Christianity up through the 1500s. It would have been acceptable to a pagan group of converts but never to traditional Jews.

The passage in Matthew of the Wise Men enabled a reliance on pseudo-science and drew the Catholic Church into incorporating theories into its moral and ethical beliefs while excommunicating those whose real science contradicted existing church dogma. The reliance on the earth as the center of the universe was basic Church doctrine. Contradicting this idea was the basis for excommunications and death. Even the belief that the perception of the movement of the stars et al. in relation to the earth engendered some form of human activity placed human behavior beyond individual accountability and rejected the notion that man may control his actions, and chose a moral life by his own free will. One of the central tenets of Judaism is that man may influence if not direct his own life by his acts of mortality or piety.

The appeal of this portion of the gospel is to a pagan audience of Asia Minor or Persia. To devout, reasonably well educated Jews in Judea or Galilea the notion of three Persian magi divining by the stars the birth of the "King of the Jews," and indirectly inducing Herod to slaughter male infants must be seen as a pagan fairy tale. To a pagan, however, it would have buttressed the image of Jesus as a figure of not only worldwide importance because of the attraction of foreign dignitaries, but the appearance in the heavens of a "star" whose meaning was interpreted and followed by a Persian magi. Not only do their gifts signify the presence of royalty but also a memorable and significant death.

The inclusion of what is essentially a pagan fairy tale into the history of Jesus, was designed to attract pagan followers whose beliefs would have already included astrology, the mystical powers of Persian sorcerers, and the relationship of an earth-oriented solar system to human events. It reinforced the belief in pseudo-science and caused the rejection of newly discovered scientific births or the theories by the Church. As such, it impeded the growth of human knowledge and prolonged the Dark Ages. It caused the excommunication of courageous thinkers. Ideas such as heliocentricity, the curvature of the earth, evolution, numerous health and medical issues, have been retarded or rejected by the pagan beliefs in pseudo-science adopted by the Church. Even today, the rejection of scientific method and the acceptance of pseudo-science is an immense political problem in countries of western civilization, who rely on literalist interpretations of the Bible.

Vicarism

RICHARD MALMED

Another dangerous myth that arises not only in Christianity but at various stages of other religions is that of vicarism – the idea that between the followers of a certain religion and God, there is a human intermediary through which any prayer or communication with God must pass. In this way, the priests control the basic theology, ritual, laws and morality and subject the peasants to conformity to the orthodox standards maintained by the Church hierarchy.

In early Judaism, the society coalesced around the idea that it was necessary to sacrifice animals to God, but only in the Temple in Jerusalem. The very scene where Jesus attacked the money changers in the Temple courtyard is one of his most dangerous and public acts. It must be understood that the Antonia Palace was where the Roman soldiers were stationed for the Passover pilgrimage. There, they could simply look over the ramparts to observe all the activities in the Temple courtyard. As we know, this act took place during the festival of Passover when the population of the city of Jerusalem swelled from 25,000 to 50,000 to over 250,000. Pontius Pilate was sufficiently concerned about civil unrest during this time that he marched two of his three legions from their customary seat at Caesarea on the coast to Jerusalem in anticipation of some form of civil unrest.

The background of the conflict had been smoldering for hundreds of years, but was coming to one of many flashpoints between 4 BCE and 135 CE. At various times the Roman legion from Caesarea, and from nearby Syria, would descend on Judea, Samaria, or Galilee and slaughter tens of thousands of Jews and crucify their leaders. Jesus' trial and crucifixion was but one of many Roman acts of brutality until the final eradication of Jewish civilization in Judea in about 135 CE.

The formula under which the Romans ruled was similar to that of Alexander the Great over 300 years previous. Once conquered, the native peoples would continue to govern themselves, maintain their existing culture and religion as long as they were peaceful and paid massive amounts of taxes to the conquerors. This was known as the Pax Romana – Roman "peace." The Jews were "a stiff-necked people," however, whom the Romans never were able to understand or control. They insisted on worshipping only one God who had no idol surrogate. They had unalterable dietary laws, inflexible rules for the Sabbath, circumcision, et. al. Their beliefs were written down from a tradition of over 1,000 years, and in written form for at least 600 years. They simply were not going to substitute their idols and Gods for similar Roman gods and idols. Their very religion dictated in detail how they ran their lives.

Sacrifice, however, was an area that was ambiguous. Many Jewish sources discounted or outright disparaged sacrifice. The banning of human sacrifice was established by the story of Abraham and his son. From this episode, it became clear that human sacrifice was forbidden. Animal sacrifice continued to persist. But 1 Samuel 15:22 asks, "Does the Lord delight in burnt offerings and sacrifices as much as in obeying the Lord? To obey is better than sacrifice, and to heed is better than the fat of rams." Psalms 51:16 "You do not delight in sacrifice, or I would bring it; you do not take pleasure in burnt offerings." Throughout the Old Testament the practice was seen as a worthless empty act derived as a vestige of the neighboring pagan tribes' religious practices. It became apparent that the act of burning animals or vegetables in a ritualistic formula by a group of hereditary priests who would feast on the remains was not meaningful to many of the Jewish thinkers. After the diaspora in 70 C.E., the Sadducees disappeared from the pages of history and the Jewish ritual of sacrifice with it.

The Jewish priesthood, the Coha'nim, was a 1,300-year-old dynasty of men descended from Aaron – Moses' brother. As the religion began to look at Jerusalem during David's reign, this line of hereditary priests began to insist on having all Jews come to Jerusalem to engage in the ritual of animal sacrifice. Extremely explicit rules were set forth in the Torah – Deuteronomy especially – to guide the priests in their garb and procedures. With the control of this franchise, this hereditary group – known as the Sadducees – were able to grow extremely wealthy from their control of the Temple and the ritual of sacrifice.

When the Romans took over Judea, they found the Sadducees were the most convenient and vulnerable group to negotiate with to maintain control over the population. The Romans, in turn, maintained tight control over the Sadducees. As a result, the Sadducees were able to maintain their comfortable positions of power and wealth with an even stronger backing from their Roman overlords over their own coreligionists.

There was a dual system of judicial administration and a dual system of taxation – one by the Romans, and a second by the Temple authorities.

Obviously, groups rose in opposition to this all-too-comfortable relationship. On the religious level, the Pharisees opposed the centralized authority of the Sadducees seated at the Temple of Jerusalem. They also took issue with much of the theology and rituals. The Pharisees were scattered throughout Judea and the Galilee, and conducted services, educated youth and did virtually everything modern day rabbis or protestant ministers do today. They performed no sacrifices. On a political level, the zealots formed guerilla-type factions to attack the Romans. The Sicarii, another form of guerrilla or terrorist type group, were known for the use of daggers with which they would attack those Jews siding with the Roman authorities. Lastly, the Essenes have traditionally been thought of as a monastic group who withdrew from society and lived in small ritualistic communities and practiced strictly defined rituals of eating, and limited sexual relations. Memberships, or following in any of these groups did not necessarily preclude membership or sympathy with any of these other groups.

In order to examine Jesus' attack against the money changers in the court of the Temple, which could be viewed by Roman soldiers from Antonia fortress, it is necessary to see that it was motivated in part by some or all of these anti-Sadducee elements.

The Temple as a center for animal sacrifice was merely duplicating what most pagan religions, not only in the Middle East, but throughout prior human existence, had done. By controlling the sacrificial ceremony, they controlled the religion which controlled the people by administering this superstitious rite. Jewish leaders and learned men for the previous millennium had repeated that sacrifice was not a necessary rite. While fiercely maintaining the Sabbath, and dietary restrictions among other strongly held beliefs, the Pharisees were quite willing to abandon sacrifice. They saw the illogic of a religious rite that offered no positive benefit except to the priesthood.

Jesus, in one short act of civil disobedience, had opened to ridicule an embarrassing fact of Sadducean corruption under the noses of their

Roman protectors. The useless and vestigial remnant of prior pagan practices, the animal sacrifice, could easily be discarded from Jewish theology. There was ample precedent. The same priests who demanded ritual purity – in diet, in Sabbath observance, in virtually every act in Jewish life – were obviously perverting a religious ceremony for their own economic benefit. As Jesus was often able to point out, empty ritual was meaningless when confronted by serious crises of health, life or death, or even simple good deeds. His parables are full of exposures of hypocritical practices and this raid on the money changers must be seen as intentionally such an act.

Many scholars have attempted to determine the precise motivation for such an obvious and risky public demonstration. Generally, there has been the suggestion that he was aligned with a group known as the Zealots who sought the military overthrow of the Roman occupation. Others believed that he and his followers had come to believe that he was the Messiah. Some believe that his attack was more motivated against the Temple authorities themselves.

Undoubtedly, Jesus sought to conform his actions to well-known prior prophecies in the Bible. After a successful but short rise to fame as a preacher in the Galilee, Jesus sought to enter an entirely new world. The area of the Galilee where Jesus had been born and raised was where his ministry had been so successful. It was a loosely defined area made up of the former kingdom of Israel which had lost power centuries before. It had become a largely ungoverned area where gangs of bandits roamed freely and attacked travelers. Most of its inhabitants were poor, and many had lost their lands to wealthy landlords who had purchased their farmsteads for back taxes and permitted the inhabitants to remain as sharecroppers. The people were viewed by the more sophisticated, wealthier people in Judea and more specifically in Jerusalem as crude country bumpkins.

For Jesus to come to Jerusalem and speak in his much-demeaned Galilean accent was an act of bravado Nonetheless, in fulfillment of the prophecy of Zecheriah, Jesus had someone procure him a donkey and a donkey colt so he could enter the gate of the city while his people spread palm fronds and sang "Hosannah" (salvation). This entry combined with his advance notice that he was descendent of the house of David, was to proclaim to all that he was intended to be viewed as the Messiah.

The Messiah as understood in Jewish culture at the time was not a diety nor necessarily a military leader. Any hint that he was somehow a god would have been viewed as an abominable heresy and dismissed out of hand as a fraud. Instead, he was expected to be a spiritual leader who would, by energizing the people to a more obedient, more observant attitude toward God, usher in a golden age, the Kingdom of God, where peace and justice would prevail.

Any suggestion that he was connected to a military group must be dismissed. Obviously, no military support ever materialized before, during or after his arrival, and his band of disciples fled at his arrest, leaving him only with his mother and Mary Magdalene to support him. No Zealots arose to support him against the Romans. Only Joseph of Arimathea, a wealthy merchant and Nicodemus, a learned Pharisean sage were present at his crucifixion.

Yet Jesus' well-planned, well-thought out attack on the money lenders was a calculated act. It was an exposure of the greed and corruption of the Sadducees and the Temple authority and it was an indirect embarrassment to the Roman rule. The practice of sacrifice had hardened into a corrupt source of income for the high priests. Superstitious pilgrims would travel great distances with their families to Jerusalem. Their animals for sacrifice had to meet very high standards of ritual purity or they would not be acceptable by the Temple authorities. These animals could not survive the long trek to Jerusalem and had to be purchased locally i.e. in the outer Temple court itself from vendors who were licensed at considerable expense by the Temple authorities. The exchange of money for these animals could not be in foreign coin but only coins minted by Jewish authorities. As a result, the legal tender derived from transactions throughout the Galilee and Judea were rarely in the local coin of Jerusalem but the currency of many nations who traded in the area. Once again, the Temple authorities would license the money changing booths to men who would in turn gouge the pilgrims in the exchange for local currency.

While many religions and communities clung to the rite of sacrifice, Judaism had many stronger elements to its religion. First, it was a religion founded on the "book" or the "word" much of which was contained in the Torah. As a foundation for interpersonal governance, it was portable and could survive any dislocation of the Temple, or the ousting of the dynasty of kings or chief priests. The religion did survive a complete exile of the population to Babylon for over 60 years in the 500s BCE. Second, it was based on the concept of one god, who was not "anthropomorphic." Jews not only believed that there was one god, but that He had a fatherly-type spirit who treated His chosen people as naughty children. He himself, unlike the pagan gods, did not have love interests, or practice incest, deceit, trickery but directed all his known or revealed interests in protecting, nurturing, scolding and disciplining His humans. Third, Judaism was not based on fertility rites, astrological cycles, or nature. Ancient peoples saw the birth and death cycles of animals and crops, or the cycles of the moon, the seasons, or the stars as a manifestation of god. As a result, there was a reliance on the inevitability of events in an ever-revolving and repeating of events. Instead the Jews developed a belief in the evolving perfection of mankind toward a world of peace.

More importantly, Jesus never seems to have sought to combat the Roman authorities. Most remembered is his famous response to the tax collector as to whether the Roman tax should be resisted. He was content to reply, "Render unto Caesar the things that are Caesar's, and unto God, the things that are God's." More than just a flippant response to avoid confrontation with the Roman authorities, it reflected the nature of his mission: to confront the Sadducean dynasty of priests in order to purify the religion.

A review of the commentary of the Dead Sea Scrolls describes the Essenes as not merely a group of monastic Jews who had withdrawn from the world to practice a communal form of ritual living with strict diet, dress, sex and marriage codes. Dispersed throughout Judea and Galilee were small communities of followers of the Essene doctrine and way of life. They circulated among the rest of the community dressed in their familiar gleaming white garments. According to the Dead Sea Scrolls, they were a younger and highly militant non-hereditary sect of Zadokite priests who sought reform of the Temple practice. As a result of current interpretation and analysis of the Dead Sea Scrolls, it appears that the Essenes dismissed the Sadducees as corrupt but had little affection for the Pharisees as well. Of course, they considered the corrupt old dynasty of Sadducees as essentially wicked and a major stumbling block to the Jews achieving the Kingdom of God by correct actions and beliefs. While these Essenes had little negative to say about the Pharisees' religious stance, they felt that they were "lovers of smooth things." That is, the Pharisees were too often willing to accept the status of things as they were and essentially concede sovereignty to the Romans and their puppets the Sadducees. While it is difficult to determine what is meant precisely in the post crucifixion portions of the Gospels of Mark 28, Luke 24 and Mark 16, there is a reference to a man or men dressed in gleaming white garments. Since in those days, the Essenes were well known as they went about dressed in white garments, it is entirely possible that the gospel writers were referring to these very Essenes. Their presence at the tomb as Mary Magdalene and the other women appeared on the third day to prepare the body for entombment must certainly be deemed as more than a suspicious coincidence, and a sign of this interest and involvement in Jesus' anti-Sadducean crusade.

Certainly there is no evidence that Jesus was either an Essene or a Zealot. As an Essene, he would have been required to engage in strict monastic habits including clothing and diet. In his missionary travels, he never did anything of the sort. He himself could not be considered either a Zealot or a member of the Sicarii. His message was one of peace and not armed violent confrontation. Jesus most violent and unambiguous act was directed at the Temple oligarchy of the hereditary Sadducee sect. It would be natural that Jesus would partake of the message of the Essenes, the younger non-hereditary Zadokite claim that the Jewish peasantry need not participate in the required rite of animal sacrifice. Not only was the practice deemed worthless and ineffectual but because of the control it had on the peasants, it interfered with their preparation for the "Kingdom of God." It was the intersession of the Sadducees between man and God to which Jesus most objected.

With the destruction of the Temple and the eventual elimination of the Sadducee sect, the rite of animal sacrifice disappeared from the Jewish religion and its later Christian offshoots. However, there remained in the Christian phase of the religion a strong presence of a requirement that the peasant seek God only through an organized and occasionally oppressive priesthood. Perhaps the strongest rites to replace animal sacrifice was that of communion and confession. In this way, a person would confess his sins to a priest who was a necessary vicarious link to God. The overpowering effect of this rite is incalculable. The priesthood in every village would know in detail the peccadillos of the entire lay population. All those who were not in a "state of grace," by attending regular confession, could not partake in communion at a weekly public mass, and thus be exposed to their fellow villagers. By this rite as well as other major issues, the Catholic Church was able to acquire immense power and wealth. They owned lands, held serfs in virtual slave-like control, had their own feudal armies, and but for the requirement of celibacy (often ignored) had all the trappings of wealth and nobility.

The strong control of the Catholic Church held the entire Western world in thrall for over a thousand years until the late 1500s when gradually cracks appeared in this power. Henry VIII of England, objected famously to his inability to get a divorce, but mainly hungered for the Church lands. By its allegiance to Rome, the Church offered him little in the way of financial or military support. Martin Luther also saw the Church hierarchy as a corrupt system selling religious favors and not observing its own commandments, as to chastity, abstemiousness and humility. Martin Luther also sought marriage for priests but his reforms otherwise, were mainly structural. In most Protestant religions, the requirement of confession and that a priest intervene – as a vicar of Christ – between the church member and God was also eliminated. The Protestants were able to read the Bible in their own language and develop a direct relationship to their concept of God.

That is not to say that the act of confession is itself bad. Quite the contrary, the benefits of examining one's life, recognizing aloud some major or minor areas that need rehabilitation, are extremely therapeutic. Having a neutral third person, who provides some feedback and some mildly invasive probing, to listen and serve as a safeguard against a welter of psychological defense mechanisms such as rationalization, projection or denial must be seen as beneficial and therapeutic. It is the control by a political entity of a communication between man and God that is an evil.

This intercession of a priestly cult between man and God was an invidious practice which began to see its last influences only in the last several centuries. The Protestant reformation was a substantial factor in this, as was the publication of the Bible in the common language. Without the strong control of the populace by the priests, the Christian world could have a more personal and meaningful relationship with God. The translation of the Gutenberg Bible into the vernacular made the scriptures available to the mass of Christians. Previously, because only the priests were educated in and literate in Latin, only they controlled access to the scriptures and their interpretation. In this way, they interposed themselves between the individual and God.

Jesus certainly saw the evils of a vicar, in the form of a dynastic priesthood who maintained a superstitious control over its adherents. The church fathers in their wisdom, however, perpetuated that control, by an entire priestly hierarchy.

The intervention of a priest or priestly class in the religious process prevented the individual practitioner from having a direct relationship with God and his own interpretation of religious experience. Jesus saw this as a pernicious influence, and condemned the practice of sacrifice controlled by the Sadducees. The latter control of the communion ceremony and the confessional by the Catholic clergy similarly exerted tremendous pressure on the peasant population. The exclusivity of the Latin language also prevented the practitioners from having access to the scriptures and their interpretation. The tight link between the church and the king, in turn, kept the population in a state of perpetual and abject servitude and ignorance for centuries. The fortuitous confluence of the Protestant reformation exposing the Church's oppressive and corrupt practices together with the publication of the Gutenberg Bible in the vernacular was able to eliminate the need to approach God or religious concepts through an intermediary vicar. In this way, the general populace were able to cast off their serfdom, and acquire independence from the oppressive feudal system.

BIRTH CONTROL AND *Masturbation*

RICHARD MALMED

Two sensitive issues in Western culture arise from cultural taboos believed to be derived from the Bible. In fact, the only reference to either birth control or masturbation in the Old Testament comes only from a misinterpretation of the acts of Onan (Gen:38) in his marriage to Tamar. The very artistically compact but dramatic tale of Tamar lays out in narrative fashion a number of strong ethnic principles of early biblical times, but in no way deals with the present sexual taboos associated with birth-control or masturbation.

In the story, Tamar in an arranged marriage, became the wife of Er, the son of Judah who was the son of Jacob and brother of Joseph, both much revered Hebraic figures. For unexplained reasons, Er died, apparently for displeasing God. It then became the duty under what is known as Levirate law for the second son Onan to marry his childless sister-in-law and have a child by her. Onan, however, was well aware that this child would receive Er's full inheritance share from Judah, and that any subsequent children by a wife of his own would divide only his share. As a result, when Onan lay with Tamar rather than impregnating her, he "spilled" his seed on the ground." (Gen 38) This act displeased God; Onan also died presumably for displeasing God leaving Tamar still childless and a widow once again. Judah was reluctant to give Tamar as wife to a third son and defaulted on his promise to Tamar's clan in their marriage pact.

Tamar's status as the now childless double widow in Judah's camp was that she would be regarded as unlucky or accursed and relegated to a position akin to a servant. Tamar was unwilling to accept this outcome and devised a plot after Judah's wife died. She is admired by Jewish authorities for her strength and ingenuity is overcoming adversity.

Accordingly, she left the camp of Judah and disguised herself as a prostitute along the trade route where her father-in-law, Judah, would travel. Judah was attracted to her and promised her a goat in return for her services. However, since he had no goat at the time, he left his seal and staff as a pledge of payment.

Three months' later, the now successfully pregnant Tamar arrived back at the family enclave. In private, she revealed the pledged seal and staff to Judah who acknowledged both the pregnancy as his and the clan's, and his default in their original marriage pact. Tamar was now recognized as Judah's wife, and given her proper status in his clan. She is further regarded favorably by Jewish Talmudic sources for her discretion in keeping her claims private and not exposing Judah to ridicule.

While today, Tamar may appear to be a loose woman and one driven by her greed to act in immoral ways like a "Hollywood starlet who sleeps her way to the top," the mores in biblical times make her a heroine for her perseverance and her insistence on her rights under the law.

The strongest motivations in these times were the preservation of the clan and the command to be fruitful and multiply. On a more practical level, most early laws had a very practical basis for their observance – the fecundity of the female was related to the economic survival of the clan. The more children, especially male children, the greater the workforce for both war and agriculture. Since battle with neighboring tribes was such a constant event, all males were trained as warriors and often would die in battle. A woman's most important contribution to the clan was to bear children to replace those lost in battle and provide a workforce for shepherding or agriculture. An infertile woman throughout the Old Testament would suffer from dishonor, and be a negative reflection on her husband. Because of frequent battles, the female population often substantially outnumbered the male. It was seen as a female's duty to resupply the clan with at least equal numbers of males and females. Tamar then was fighting to fulfill the most important duty of womanhood and preserve her role as a productive member of the community.

Females were also, in practical terms, a valuable political asset. When one tribe arranged a marriage with another, it obviously drew the two closer together and made for many economic and political benefits. The two could trade back and forth, exchange skills, interbreed herds, but more importantly, aid each other in military confrontations.

Accordingly, we must see Tamar's marriage contract as being an extremely meaningful tie between the two clans. As the weaker of the two sexes, the female was to be accorded several rights in the marriage contract. Certainly, her children would inherit their father's share. She, however, was given the elevated status as the wife of a son of the clan, and not that of subsequent or junior wife or concubine. She would thus have the ability to direct the household, the junior women, the servants, and make the decisions in all aspects of home life. (See Proverbs 31). This was the guarantee she received from the head of the clan owed to her own father and her previous clan. Defaults or violations of the marriage contracts were not taken lightly by the woman's original clan.

When we see that her marriage to Er ended in his death without children, a very important force known as the Levirate Law came into play. The brother-in-law was required to marry the childless widow of his brother and give her offspring. Onan defaulted on that sacred legal obligation and, for that, displeased God and died. He had defaulted on the principle that generating offspring is a sacred duty, and breached his clan's obligation in the marital contract.

In doing so, Onan acted out of greed – to preserve his share of the inheritance for his own children without being diminished by a share due to Tamar and her child. His sin was not practicing birth control or engaging in an immoral sexual act, but in breaching the marital contract his tribe owed to Tamar and in not producing a child to add to the tribes' manpower. By itself sexual acts were not considered sinful in those days, only ones which breached marital contracts such as adultery or rape.

Tamar, on the other hand, must be seen as a courageous enterprising woman. Rather than accept what fate has handed her by the male community or accept the impermissible violation of her marital contract, she resorted to her own intellect and personal grit to claim the life that she and her tribe had bargained for and were entitled to. In terms of the early Old Testament, she not only achieved her place in the tribe by bearing, as it turns out, twins, she is given a high place in Jewish history. One of her twins, Perez (by Judah), is the ancestor of King David, perhaps the greatest Jewish figure in history. Jesus, himself, and the New Testament claim he was descended from David, and thus Tamar (Ruth 4:18-22). It is also part of the Ethiopian tradition that Perez became King of Persia.

Neither the writer of this episode in the Old Testament, nor Onan ever believed that he was transgressing any sexual law. It is clear that his sole motivation was greed for a share of his father's inheritance undiminished by his deceased and childless brother's share. He had violated the Levirate Law – which required a man to marry and beget a child by his deceased brother if he died childless. The purpose of the law is obvious: To take advantage of the excess population of females in aiding in the propagation of the tribe and to uphold the terms of the marital contract of the deceased brother's tribe and, thus, satisfy the concerns of her family for her future well-being. Otherwise, there is no mention of any disapprobation of birth control, per se, or masturbation. Of course, birth control would have been viewed as contrary to the directive to be fruitful and multiply, or, in other words, enrich the population of the clan by providing healthy offspring. Since the value of a large family has diminished in today's world, especially after Thomas Malthus has so adeptly warned, of excess population, we are now concerned with overpopulation rather than the reverse. We must consider today's attitudes concerning masturbation and birth control to be ones not derived from the Bible at all, but from some other, possibly Pauline, aversion to sex itself.

The New Testament and principally words attributed to Paul assign guilt to the taboos associated with birth control and masturbation. Paul had a substantial dislike for women, marriage and sexual intercourse which the Jews of the Old Testament and Jesus simply did not have. It is Paul's, or those persons writing for Paul or claiming to be Paul, who made these sexual taboos part of the Christian doctrine and, as a result, western culture.

The concept of some aspects of sex as sin arose for the first time in the Pauline aspects of Christianity. Later, it was claimed that Jesus was celibate and, since good Christians should imitate Jesus, they too should abstain from sex. However, there is no support in any of the gospels that Jesus either abstained from sex, was never married or encouraged others to do likewise.

The disapprobation of masturbation or birth control is simply not dealt with in the Old Testament or by Jesus in the New Testament, and the story of Onan is simply not support for any such interpretation.

Next Chapter

ROMAN TRIAL

ROMAN *Trial*

RICHARD MALMED

From the Gospels, it is apparent that Jesus was taken into custody on Passover eve, about midnight, and spent the early morning hours thereafter in the home of the father-in-law of the High Priest Caiaphas. This proceeding whatever it was, dealt only with Jewish law. Jesus was then delivered to the Roman authorities for a determination of what would occur under roman law whether for a trial of some sort by Pilate, or some other procedure. It had been suggested in Luke 23 that Pilate did not take up the case immediately, but sent Jesus to Herod Antipas for his determination. For whatever reason, Antipas refused to accept the trial of Jesus and returned him promptly to Pilate. We then know that Jesus was tried before Pilate by about 9:00 am. At which time Pilate determined in very short order that he should be crucified immediately and Jesus died on the cross in the very short time of six hours afterwards. This then is the timeline for the Roman phase of Jesus' trial under Roman auspices.

The Gospel in John 19, relates that an angry mob of Jews assembled in a location where they could be heard by Pilate, and insisted that the Romans crucify him for an act which had offended some unspecified factions in the Jewish community. As a result, a timid and indecisive Pilate, pressured by Jewish interests, ordered that Jesus by crucified but "washed his hands" of the decision.

From the timeline alone, it is difficult to believe this analysis. The early morning hours of Passover day, following the Passover feast, would not have attracted many people to the Antonia Palace, where Jesus had been taken. The Sadducees, the Temple priests, had to conduct sacrifices for about 250,000 pilgrims and perform many other ceremonies and services during that day. The pilgrims themselves would have been standing in long lines awaiting their opportunity to sacrifice. Of all elements in the Jewish community that had the greatest quarrel with Jesus, the Sadducees should have been the most vocal. Jesus had entered their Temple area and overturned the money changers' tables and disrupted the sacrifice procedure that was taking place. Assuming about 250,000 pilgrims had come to Jerusalem for the main purpose of having the Sadducee priests conduct a sacrifice for them, Jesus' act of civil disobedience was intended to embarrass and point up the meretricious and hypocritical institution that the Temple priests had fostered. Yet the Sadducees would have been too busy with their holiday functions to appear in the early morning hours.

The possibility that a large crowd had assembled by about 9:00 a.m. on Passover day must be discounted by the very design of the fortress with high walls where the trial of Jesus before Pilate would have occurred. There is a conflict over whether the Praetorium was located in the Antonia Palace or the Jerusalem Palace erected by Herod and then occupied by his son Herod Antipas. Either palace was constructed as a military fortress and certainly invulnerable to a crowd of ordinary protesters. Each palace had walls about 13 to 16 feet in height and were built on elevated platforms of rock over 500 to 1,000 feet to command views of the surrounding city. Antonia Palace shared a wall with the Temple and had towers 75 to 100 feet in height designed to give the soldiers on duty a view of the activities in the adjoining Temple court.

The gospels all refer to the Praetorium where Pilate conducted the trial. John 18:28, Matt. 27:27, Mark 15:16. Pilate would have been seated on a sella – a throne-like chair, in a room known as the secretorium, which as the name implies was a location which was private or secret. His only attendants would have been "apparitores" or official observers and clerks writing down orders or recording his proceedings.

The possibility that a crowd of whatever size, especially one assembled at 9:00 am on the Passover holiday, could have been heard or created some influence on Pilate is unrealistic. It is also unrealistic that Pilate would have exposed himself or his troops to a crowd when he was conducting the trial of a possible Jewish insurgent. It should be noted that Jesus was from Galilee – the region in the north which had been the birthplace of several previous uprisings. Undoubtedly the pilgrims would have had many Galileans in their midst, some of whom may have had rebellious leanings.

It is important to remember that Jesus was a Jew preaching a reasonably acceptable Jewish message. As he said, he came to uphold the law not to change it. Doctrines that he was divine, or the Son of God, do not begin to appear until at last 20 years after his death. Even so, claiming to be God or a god was not punishable by death or even a crime under Jewish law. Saying the actual name of God out loud was blasphemy. It is debatable whether Jesus claimed to be the Messiah or even the King of the Jews, but neither of these was a crime. The debate over whether Jesus was divine lasted for several centuries and was only finally resolved by the Nicaean Creed in 325 CE at Constantine's convocation of favored church officials; Those with differing doctrines were silenced, or killed off. In short, there were no witnesses or evidence produced that would have served to convict Jesus of a crime under Jewish law.

It is also important to note that the Roman trial sought out entirely different issues from the Jewish one. Doctrinal purity, obedience to Jewish law, and blasphemy, were entirely irrelevant to the Romans. Pontius Pilate had only two directives from Rome: Keep the peace and bring in tax revenues. At the time, the relatively poor regions of Judea and Galilee were sufficiently unruly to require three Roman legions to suppress Jewish opposition to its rule. It also required the surrounding Roman colonies in Syria and Egypt to remain on alert to quell any uprising. On the other hand, because of its relative poverty, it produced well below its expected tax revenues. While the Romans were tolerant of the religious practices of its previous pagan conquests, it could not understand or tolerate those of the Jews, who were extremely adamant about their beliefs and were the only conquered peoples to enter into combat or rebellion in order to maintain their religion without Roman interference. Pagan religions followed formats and rituals similar to those of Rome. A local pantheon would normally include physical objects or idols which represented qualities found in nature: the sun, the moon, bulls, water, female fertility, weather and only occasionally abstract qualities such as wisdom or beauty. The worship of these gods consisted of sacrifices at their respective temples to request the beneficial influence these gods were believed to have control over, usually fertility, good weather, bountiful harvests. In each pagan town, there was usually a temple to one or more of the gods, with specific dates for ritual holidays. The Romans would assume control over the towns, and soon to follow would be Roman priests of one god or another. With little difficulty, the local pagan townspeople could change allegiance to the Roman gods who corresponded closely to their local deities. There was little resistance to Roman influence in the area of religious principles.

The Jews, however, had demonstrated a willingness to fight over its principles of monotheism, the Sabbath, graven images or idols, and control of its Temple. On the one hand, the Romans, as part of its requirements of conquest, insisted on the right to select the high priest of the Temple who would thus be beholden to the Roman governor for his continuing rights and privileges. In this way, the Sadducees, the hereditary line of high priests who controlled the activities of the Temple and Temple sacrifice, under which they had become the wealthy elite of Jerusalem, and could easily be persuaded to be compliant with Roman demands. Nonetheless, uprisings occurred with surprising frequency. On one occasion, Roman images of Tiberius, the then Caesar were displayed at the Temple. The image of a human worshipped as a deity by the Romans and set up for public view near the Temple was an abomination under Jewish law forbidding the worship of idols. After a heated confrontation but no violence, the Romans were persuaded to remove the offending symbols.

By virtue of his other rulings prior to Jesus' trial, it must be assumed that Pilate neither knew nor cared much about Jewish culture. His imposition of a number of likenesses of Tiberius around the Temple could be seen as either a deliberate affront or an inept act which provoked the Jewish population. His theft or expropriation of Temple funds to build an aqueduct and his later slaughter and crucifixion of thousands of Samaritans for conducting a religious ceremony, all along with other insensitive and brutal acts, must be taken to characterize Pilate as neither a squeamish nor vacillating governor. Thus, when confronted with a rabble-rousing preacher during Passover whom neither the Jews, nor Herod Antipas, would punish, he could no longer avoid responsibility. His confrontation with Jesus could only have taken, at most, a few hours, at least, a few minutes.

Under normal circumstances, a Roman criminal defendant might have been entitled to a number of rights including a public trial, the appearance and confrontation of eyewitnesses, not merely hearsay ones, and a lawyer. In the short time between the arrest and trial, Jesus was given none of those rights.

Pilate had first given what he thought was the Jewish Sanhedrin and possibly Antipas the opportunity to deal with Jesus. Perhaps he felt he could duck responsibility for punishing a popular preacher. It must be seen that he took a risk in doing so. If either had chosen to conduct a trial at some point in the future under the strict provisions of Jewish law, it might have given time for factions to coalesce around Jesus as the witnesses failed to come forward with any credible evidence of a crime. Perhaps he felt he was on thin ice with Rome for his past acts of brutality. Nonetheless he was saddled with full responsibility for this Galilean upstart.

Pilate must have seen that the situation must be dealt with quickly and decisively. There was an overwhelming number of people in Jerusalem at the time, some of whom may have been zealots – guerilla warriors dedicated to ousting Roman rule. A public trial, or a delay might have given courage to such a group. A swift brutal solution to the problem would disabuse any dissidents of an armed insurrection. Nothing would discourage a crowd faster than having its potential leader slowly dying in agony and then having his face and body picked at by birds while it rotted in plain view on a major highway.

Clearly Pilate opted for his authority to assert martial law and conduct by himself in secret an interrogation to be followed by immediate crucifixion. If, as has been suggested, he had any doubts, or wished to divine the temper of the people, he could easily have subjected Jesus to a trial under appropriate Roman law with a duly appointed judge.

The next consideration is what issues did Pilate consider. Jesus had not attacked Rome or interfered with the Pax Romana directly. He had staged a public protest against the Sadducees and their sacrifice ritual, but, when confronted by obvious provocateurs, he refused to encourage people to default on their taxes, but urged that they "render unto Caesar, that which is Caesar's." In doing so, he referred to the obvious idolatry of Caesar's image on the coins themselves. Certainly, Jesus was reputed to be of the Davidic royal blood line. This claim must be seen as spurious when claimed in Matthew and Luke where the bloodline ran through Joseph's ancestors'. While, at the same time, the Gospel claimed that Mary had been impregnated by the Holy Spirit, rendering Joseph irrelevant to the birth process.

However, David and Solomon had many wives and concubines and as a result many children. Their successors in the bloodline also had many children over the next 50 or so generations. Thousands of males could claim the right to the Davidic royal line. Yet Pilate's conclusion was that Jesus "of Nazareth" sought to be the "King of the Jews."

Only 100 years before the Jews had been ruled by the Hasmoneans better known as the Maccabees who lead a guerrilla uprising to defeat the Greek-led Assyrians and reclaim Judean independence. The Romans were well aware of this because they had been peaceably invited into Judea to settle a claim between two subsequent claimants to the Hasmonean throne. The Romans, as events played out, gained control over Judea without a fight, but the knowledge of the prior fierce Jewish warriors expelling the Assyrians was something they could not ignore.

The interest of Pilate then would have been sharply focused on security to defuse a possibly incipient uprising during Passover weekend. He had to see Jesus as a clear and present danger. But what would have suggested that Jesus presented such a threat, and what would have caused him to mock Jesus by placing a sign saying "King of the Jews" on his cross. There must have been some intelligence that the Romans had uncovered that suggested that Jesus was connected to the rebel group – the Zealots. At his trial, Jesus is only asked if he is the "King of the Jews," he replies that only others say this. It can be implied from his answer either that other people falsely say this or that he is, but will not admit it directly.

Jesus, if we can oversimplify by interpreting his words, sought the Kingdom of God – a time when justice would prevail, the meek would inherit the earth, and there would be peace. He was speaking of a religious vision he had which could be brought about by men upholding the Jewish law, avoiding sin and atoning for past transgressions, and above all worshipping the one true God. Pilate who had little interest in Jewish culture, misinterpreted this message and believed Jesus sought temporal power by means of force by defeating the Romans militarily. But, by itself, this Galilean preacher with a ragtag bunch of followers, who had until then only gathered a following in Galilee, the home of what those in Judea thought were unlettered bumpkins, would have instilled little fear in Pilate. He could have given Jesus a public whipping and sent him back to Galilee with his tail between his legs where he would have been viewed a deluded simpleton.

Pilate had to have believed that there was some other connection between Jesus and the Zealots. We are certainly aware that Peter and other disciples carried swords and acted as Jesus' bodyguards, and that they carried nicknames that sounded vaguely like noms de guerre – Boanerges, or Sons of Thunder (Mark 3:17). – false names that they assumed for their roles as guerilla warriors. However, the one disciple that stands out that may have "betrayed" Jesus connection to the Zealots is Judas Iscariot. As his name implies he was a member of the "Sicarii" – a group of guerilla warriors who killed Romans or Roman collaborators with a short dagger known as a sicar. Judas, unlike the rest of Jesus' followers, was not Galilean, but came from Jerusalem. The difference between a Galilean accent and a Judean one was particularly remarkable to any Judean who regarded Galileans as uneducated country bumpkins. The Romans regarded Galileans as the source of past uprisings and the birthplace of many would-be rebel leaders.

As the governor of a difficult region and the commander of several legions, Pilate undoubtedly had been briefed on the possibilities of Jesus' mission as one of provoking a violent revolt. It is no wonder that Pilate would discount Jesus' actual words defining his mission - the apocalyptic kingdom of God and deduce that Jesus was the spiritual leader of an armed group seeking the return of an actual kingdom of the Jews.

Pilate, a brutal and insensitive governor was charged with keeping the peace in Jerusalem during a time when the city could be viewed as particularly combustible because of the enormous influx of pilgrims, many of whom would be Galilean. So, it is wholly appropriate to draw the conclusion that Pilate acted alone in condemning Jesus to crucifixion in a quick and decisive exercise of the powers of martial law.

It is possible to conclude that the presence of several possible Zealots in Jesus' entourage provided the intelligence necessary for the Romans to determine that Jesus' aim was armed rebellion leading to a return of Judea to Jewish control. Although Simon Zelotes, and the Boanerges were in his company, perhaps the most damning of disciples was Judas Iscariot. Judas with his Judean accent and frequent trips back and forth to the disciples, appeared most likely to have a connection to the Zealots. In this way, it may be said that Judas "betrayed" Jesus. Perhaps that is what was meant in the back and forth conversation between Jesus and Judas during the Passover feast. Judas made Jesus aware of his possible exposure, and Jesus encouraged Judas to continue to do what he felt was the inevitable course of events. Escape and the abandonment of his ministry in Judea was always a possibility. Yet Jesus appears to have intentionally put himself in harm's way despite Judas' warning.

On the other hand, Jesus may actually have had a war-like intent which Pilate correctly interpreted. It is difficult to ignore the presence of not only Judas, but Simon Zelotes and James and John, the sons of Zebedee (Mark 3:17) the Boanerges. Jesus himself said, "Think not I am come to send peace on earth; I am not to send peace, but a sword." (Matt. 10:34). He also said, "He that hath no sword, let him sell his garment and buy one." (Luke 22:36). The name Barabbas also appears in the gospels as the one to be released in place of Jesus and in accordance with the Jewish crowds' wishes; but there is no recorded instance of the Jews having a tradition where they released a prisoner. Jesus was crucified along with two "lestai," translated as bandits or thieves but this was a term the Romans used for Jewish rebels. The name Barabbas should actually be Bar Abbas, meaning son of the father. It was extremely likely that this was a nom de guerre or the leadership title of a rebel leader. It certainly was not a common name. This picture becomes clearer when it is shone that the Romans had ample evidence that Jesus associated with Zealots and Judas in particular and were not merely peaceful, itinerant healers and preachers. Pilate then can be justified for believing that Jesus and the other two lestai intended armed rebellion and deserved a very public and painful death on the cross for those considering armed rebellion to see. Jesus' "trial" then was only an interrogation prior to a summary disposition under martial law for his crucifixion along with other possible rebels.

NEXT CHAPTER

MONOTHEISM

Monotheism

RICHARD MALMED

Abraham is noted as the first man to abandon idols, and believe in monotheism. The religions before that believed in multiple gods each of whom represent some part of human experience. Nature, the stars, and different animals were worshipped for the qualities they had and could, it was believed, confer on humans who worshipped them and offered them sacrifices, great benefits. There was no moral code attached to this worship. Frequently the pagan gods engaged in a number of atrocities such as rape, murder, gluttony, drunkenness, deceit, theft and did not advise humans not to do so. There was to be a quid pro quo if the specific god was praised and sacrificed to, he would reward the human with fertility, good harvests, health, etc. depending on what that particular god had to offer.

The single Jewish God insisted on a moral course of action by a covenant with the people who followed his dictates. His ways were unknowable and his being was neither in idol form, nor a human form; but an indefinable type of spirit which influenced human events based on the moral sanctity of the human. In the Jewish Bible, he is seen both as a benevolent custodian, and a fierce father figure, depending on the specific human activity he reacted to.

When the early Christians adopted the belief in a trinity and considered a male in human form to be a divine son of the father God and his equal, in some mystical way his actual being, they had begun to recreate polytheism.

With the veneration of Mary, the mother of Jesus, a female form of the divinity had been created. Although unsupported by many references in the New Testament, Mary is worshipped for her purity and piety. Other than the Immaculate Conception of Jesus, she is believed to have been a virgin throughout her life. In reality, the New Testament is clear that Jesus had four other brothers and some sisters, including James the Just. However, Mary is prominently displayed throughout Christendom in many Catholic churches on a par with Jesus.

Saints are also venerated as if divine in many Catholic churches. Attributes and symbols or iconography are associated with the various saints in accordance with the lives they led or their means of death or martyrdom. Chapels abound in the cathedrals where these saints may be worshipped and asked for various things – cures for disease, fertility, safety, prosperity, etc. Often, it was easy to convert pagans, because they could substitute their gods for the saints, according to the attributes of each saint. Relics or pieces of the deceased saints are also worshipped as well as statues or paintings of the saints.

This proliferation of divine physical symbols for veneration revives many of the ills of idolatry. Each god-like figure depicted in physical form is asked for a material benefit simply through the mechanism of prayer. Often, candles are purchased for a small sum from the church and lit as part of the prayer. This small token of supplication is a vestige of the ritual of animal sacrifice.

The problem with idolatry is twofold. First, it "anthropomorphizes" God by making him fixed as a physical object for one, and as a human image for two. It imposes human limitations on his ability to act and limits his actions to the physical world. If it is believed that God is an abstract concept and He acts in the spiritual world as well as the physical, His strength and power is in the realm of human motivation and not just physical actions. To limit His power to the physical world in areas such as weather, fertility, prosperity diminishes his reach. If instead He is able to affect changes in the spheres of the spirit, or the mind, His breadth is far greater and more effective. Further, the ability of mankind to grasp abstract ideas and entertain ideas in the spiritual or mental realm expands its grasp.

The belief in the efficacy of a physical external object, or the reliance on an anthropomorphized God removes from mankind the responsibility for its own actions. It becomes possible to blame these objects or deities for one's sins and attributes gains or benefits to their power. As such, it removes from man the responsibility or reward for his own actions. The existence of one omniscient God who can observe and interpret each human's acts, but who permits that individual to choose his own action, places salvation solely in the hands of each person.

In a similar manner, the sufferings or martyrdom of the Jews or the saints is believed to relieve humans of their own guilt and offer salvation without any affirmative acts of atonement or good works on their part. Again, it removes from man the responsibility for his own acts and removes demands on his free will.

NEXT CHAPTER

JUDEO-CHRISTIAN TRADITION

Judeo-Christian TRADITION

RICHARD MALMED

Gentiles are fond of referring to a Judeo-Christian tradition. In reality, because of the teachings of Paul, there is little in early Christianity which in any way was derived from Judaism.

The tradition of Judaism rests primarily on the Torah, the Haftarah and the Mishnah. The Torah contains the first five books "of Moses." The Haftarah contains the balance of the Jewish Bible, what gentiles refer to as the Old Testament. The Mishnah contains commentary, debate, interpretation of the Torah and Haftarah collected from several hundred years prior to 600 BCE and then recorded in written form in two different versions thereafter. The Torah and Haftarah can be seen as case studies of human behavior which, in their terse narrative from illustrated situations, cast as favorable or unfavorable the acts of human beings by their subsequent divine retribution or reward. Portions of the Torah and Haftarah are read in synagogue on a revolving basis each of the 52 weeks of the year and then commented on in a sermon which interprets the weekly portion. In this way, the Jewish community is instructed to follow a moral life and repent previous errors. Over the centuries, interpretations of the Bible have been accumulated and debated back and forth.

Jews have never actively sought converts and put those desiring to convert to a rigorous education before accepting them into the religion. During the time of Jesus, there were, however, numerous sympathizers who while not considered complete in their acceptance of the faith, were nonetheless welcome into the synagogue and its activities.

The Jews were known as "the people of the book" because they relied so heavily on the written word, and a collection of moral tales with debating commentary over the centuries. In an attempt to regulate the Jewish communities, there were numerous laws, advices and teachings contained in the Torah. The sages count 613 of these which deal with all phases of human behavior, commerce, family matters, religious observance, rituals, etc. As a result, Jewish men were required to acquire some degree of literacy, and had to be able to read portions of the Torah and Haftarah as part of their Bar Mitzvah training.

After the return of the Jews from Babylonian exile, a group of rabbis known as Pharisees began to settle in each of the towns throughout Palestine and in the Jewish communities scattered throughout the

Mediterranean and Europe. Some estimates claim that over 40 percent of the Jewish population lived outside Judea and Galilee. These Pharisees assumed the roles of teaching the children and conducting services on a regular basis. The Pharisees were known for their particular insistence on strict observance of the laws, and perhaps, were over zealous in following of the many rituals.

Paul changed all that. He actively sought converts to what he at the time thought was a different sect within Judaism. Not only did he not require the pagans of Asia Minor and Greece to go through the Jewish conversion process, he eliminated the Torah, the Haftarah, the Mishnah, the 18 customary benedictions from the Jewish weekly service and the 613. Most importantly, he considered the belief in what he deemed to be the essential elements of Jesus to be more important than the teachings of correct moral behavior and repentance for past sins found throughout the Torah, Haftarah and Mishnah. He frequently railed against "the law" by which he meant the accumulated body of Jewish knowledge. These elements of belief were the divine nature of Jesus as the actual son of God, his death and resurrection, and the salvation of true believers in the afterlife. To Jews, this was an entirely different religion. To gentile converts to Christianity, it was a religion founded by prophecy and tradition in the "Old Testament" but seen more clearly in the New. As it developed, Paul's religion became unrecognizable to Jews.

By eliminating the Torah et. al., the early Christian was relying solely on the words of Jesus in the gospels, and ignoring the 1,000 years of scholarship on moral themes in the Torah. Judaism was based on a reference to past scholarship. Jesus was interpreted to look within and determine a moral course of action by what was similar to a platonic means at arriving at correct action by reasoning. He thought that faith alone would guide a Christian to correct action.

Sexual behavior became a new form of sin. Paul's direction to avoid or minimize sexual activity were entirely new to his version of Christianity. Paul derived this from his version of faith that Jesus was celibate. Although there is no evidence for such a belief, Paul himself was celibate and averse to contact with women. On the other hand, Jews considered sexual activity to be a gift from God to be enjoyed under appropriate circumstances. A brief reading of the Song of Songs will show both men's and women's voices engaged in erotic counterpoint.

Of course, inappropriate sex was deemed to be incest, bestiality, rape, and adultery. Fornication outside of marriage per se was not sinful. The Torah makes no comment on espoused Christian beliefs against birth control or masturbation. Similarly Jesus makes no such comment. Modern Catholics find both sinful.

The true Judeo-Christian tradition does not begin to arise until after the Protestant Reformation when scholars began to read Hebrew and re-discover the tradition of the Old Testament, the Jewish Bible. There they discovered that a system of laws could be developed where a reference to past rulings and the interpretation of existing laws would lead to a more predictable system of governance. In England, the decisions by judges based on prior well-reasoned principles were collected and referred to, for newly litigated matters. The system known as "stare decisus," i.e. to stand decided, is the foundation of the British and American legal systems. It is these prior cases to which lawyers refer, and judges weigh heavily, in reaching hopefully consistent decisions. With these predictable results in lawsuits – civil or criminal – the rights of all citizens are then protected. No litigant would be subject to a judge's personal view of his faith, but on proven reliance on previous consistent decisions. A member of an unpopular minority in a lawsuit may receive the same result in a case as the majority, ruling elite. Today's back history of case law and decisions is a close relative of the Torah, Haftarah and Mishnah, which had been neglected for 1,500 years during the Middle Ages by the ruling dynasties of church and state.

With Paul's early impetus and the early Church's rapprochement to Rome, the two religions became widely divergent. Judaism required knowledge of and obedience to the law of Moses, the Torah, the Mishnah and respect for a tradition of over 600 years in building a legal foundation, Christianity required "sola fide," only faith, in the belief of Jesus' resurrection and divinity. The priests were guided by principles of faith and love, but otherwise unguided by strong legal bases. They tended to make their advice based on ad hoc faith-based thinking. The Christians, believing their entire reward lay in the afterlife, pursued beliefs in self - sacrifice, sexual abstention, denial of pleasures of the flesh; Jews enjoyed sex, wine and other physical pleasures as God-given gifts to be enjoyed moderately within the bounds of their law.

Christians supported the divine right of kings, the union of church and state with the church controlling the peasants in a state of feudal servitude. Christians were taught that the Jews killed Jesus and were forever damned. As a result, Jews were herded into ghettos restricted in their professions and frequently subjected to attacks by the peasantry. Only the intercession of Augustine saved the Jews because he felt that they should remain as a remnant as witnesses to Jesus.

What Christians really mean by Judeo-Christian tradition is the notion 1) that, because the Jews had breached their covenant with God, they were no longer "chosen" but Christians inherited their status because they believed in God's son, Jesus; 2) that the Old Testament foreshadowed by numerous citations the superiority and subsequent accession of Christianity. As a result, the sermons, treatises and letters of the Christian Church cite, mostly out of context, parts of the Old Testament which appear to predict elements of the life of Jesus or the Christian Church. The primary one concerns an obscure passage of Jeremiah in which an "almah" will give birth to a child who shall be called Immanuel. An almah in Aramaic simply means a young woman, but has been translated into Greek to mean a virgin and thus supports the concept of Mary's virgin birth. A virgin in Aramaic is a "betulah." Obviously, the translator was either not versed enough in Aramaic or obstinately ignored the correct meaning. References abound which similarly attempt to relate the Old Testament to events in the New.

Accordingly, when Christians refer to the Judeo-Christian tradition, they mean that they consider the Old Testament a superseded source for the New and an essentially irrelevant series of stories and collections of law and moral teachings which have no meaning to them. As a result, the term "Judeo-Christian" tradition is an insult to the Jews, but often cited by Christians to suggest blandly that there is an affinity between the two, when, in fact, their core belief is that their religion not only has superseded that of Judaism, but rendered it irrelevant as well. The Jews consider that the Judeo-Christian tradition is one essentially similar to our modern legal system which uses prior case law and judicial rulings to create a built up series of predictable principles on which humans can rely. In this way, the personal feelings of the judiciary have no effect on their rulings, and the system of accumulating legal precedents gives the citizenry comfort in the way to conduct their lives.

NEXT
CHAPTER

The *Pauline* DIVERTION

RICHARD MALMED

Paul inserted some of the most dangerous myths into the center of western thinking. Virtually all of his influence came entirely out of his own inspiration with little influence from Jesus, or Judaism. In fact, the key elements of his doctrine were often directly contrary to Jesus' teaching or Jewish tradition, and usually were comingled with contemporaneous pagan practices to make pagan conversion more palatable.

Paul was born in Tarsus – a wealthy port town in what is now Southeastern Turkey. He claims to have been a Pharisee, but little is known of his education – especially his immersion in actual Jewish law. In his various letters, he betrays a lack of knowledge of actual Jewish law or history, or merely ignores it.

Paul himself was a contradiction in many ways, some of which he himself may have fostered to help spread his doctrine. On the one hand, he was a Roman citizen and a self-confessed spy or persecutor of the traditional Jewish population or the apostles of Jesus. It is also curious as to why or how Paul became a Roman citizen. The biblical texts say he inherited it from his father, but nowhere is it explained how a Jew attained this status. He may have earned it from his activities as a spy. Nevertheless, he purported to become the most ardent advocate for the promotion of Jesus or rather his definition of Jesus.

Paul never knew Jesus and did not convert to becoming a preacher on what he contended was a religion based on Jesus until about 5 to 10 years after Jesus' death. He claimed that this conversion took place on the road to Damascus where he was sent to spy on behalf of the Romans on the disciples who had fled Jerusalem. One version of this conversion appears in Acts and is told by Luke - not the disciple of Jesus, but a follower of Paul who was writing a kind of eulogy after Paul's death some thirty to forty years after Paul died. In that version, Paul was struck by a blinding light and in a vision saw Jesus and thereupon converted to the Jesus movement. He traveled on to Damascus where his blindness was cured by a member of the Jesus movement named Ananias, and baptized into the Jesus movement. Paul's own version of his conversion written about 20 years after the crucifixion is dramatically different. He attests to no such blinding vision, but does claim to have witnessed the risen Jesus for himself and, thus, claimed to be equal if not superior to the other apostles solely on the strength of a never fully delineated communication he received from Jesus.

In some places, it is popularly suggested that Paul acquired his name when he was converted to being a follower of Jesus. That is not correct. Paul is simply the Greek version of the Aramaic name Saul. As Paul addressed mostly Greek gentile groups he used the name Paul. When speaking to Jewish groups, his name was Saul.

Paul in many respects is difficult to pin down on many issues and is seen to have changed his position on what he preached or had communicated to him by Jesus, depending on which audience he addressed. As he famously said, "I have made myself a slave to everyone to win as many as possible. To the Jews, I became a Jew to win the Jews. To those under the law I became like one under the law (though I am not myself under the law) so as to win those under the law. To those not having the law I became like one not having the law (though I am not free from God's law but am under Christ's law) so as to win those not having the laws... I have become all things to all people so that by all means possible I might save some... 1 Cor 19-23.

Almost exclusively, he directed his activities to what is today Syria, Turkey and Greece, and mostly to the non-Jews or gentiles. His message was basically that it was not necessary to follow the laws of the Jews or become a Jew in order to be a follower of Jesus. In virtually every document attributed to him, Paul unrelentingly reviled not only the Jesus movement in Jerusalem which kept to the Jewish laws, but all Jews who never became associated with Jesus. He demeaned the Jewish laws and traditions at every opportunity and said that it is not necessary to follow Jewish law or tradition to be a follower of Jesus.

The historical version of Jesus that nearly all authorities on the life of Jesus, whether Jewish or Christian, is that Jesus was preaching an essentially traditional Jewish doctrine. Jesus himself said, "I have not come to change the law but to fulfill it." He never would have accepted the elimination of 1,200 years of Jewish law and tradition in the Torah, or absolved his followers from following it. It is true that Jesus occasionally ran afoul of strict Pharisaic interpretations of the law by not adhering strictly to their often heavily ritualized interpretation of Jewish law. On one occasion, he permitted his men to glean leftover grain from a field on the Sabbath. When reproached for this, he, in traditional Jewish fashion, confronted them with a legalistic argument by citing precedents from the Torah or logic (Matthew 5, Luke 6) But he never sought to call the validity of the Torah into dispute, but in a healthy Jewish tradition, debated the interpretation of the law to demonstrate that hungry men could glean on the Sabbath.

It is necessary to understand just what the Jewish law and tradition was and how it developed over 1,200 years. While the Ten Commandments are the central part of the law, there are 613 other laws throughout the Torah, as well as numerous tales which illustrate how and why these laws are to be interpreted. For this reason, Jews were referred to as the people of the book. By this, it was meant that they had a structure and purpose to their daily lives and when in doubt on complex matters could consult learned men who would apply the facts of their particular dilemma to the precedent set forth in the Torah, and its various commentaries.

The Torah and the other books of the Old Testament were not the only elements of Jewish legal and religious traditions which Paul sought to eliminate. The Talmud is a very important series of commentaries on the Torah and elsewhere. Since it began as an oral collection of biblical interpretations, its beginning is difficult to date but it certainly preceded the Babylonian exile, where most of the Jewish elite – intellectuals, doctors, merchants, etc. were forcibly deported in 598 BCE to Babylon from Jerusalem. The Persians in 538 BCE permitted their return. It is possible to see references to the Babylonian exile in the Talmud. The commentaries cover a wide range of subjects – much deals with very close textual analysis of stories of the Old Testament, but some deal with moral codes, health and hygiene, sex, marriage, community, relations and commerce. After the destruction of the Temple by the Romans in about 70 CE, two groups began to reduce the collection to written form in two schools – one in 200 CE, the other in 500 CE. Over the centuries during the diaspora, scholars continued to comment and debate on the issues raised up to the present day. In many ways, the entire Talmudic tradition is very similar to the way American and English law is created, preserved and enforced today that is called the Judeo-Christian tradition. A judge will confront a set of facts and apply reasoning from previous case law or enacted statutes to the facts in the case before him and write an opinion which displays in detail his reasoning and the previous cases he relied on to reach his conclusion. In preaching to the gentiles, Paul, by encouraging a disregard for "the law," was not only referring to the lessons and laws of the Old Testament, but also the entire Talmudic tradition. The term Judeo-Christian tradition then is a misnomer. It was actually the English who revived the tradition of using legal precedents to define the law and apply it to the legal system in the 1400s.

Instead, Paul and those writing in his tradition, believed that proper action could be derived by intuition or "knowing oneself " by deep introspection or mystical practices, by eschewing the material world – i.e. abstaining from sex, alcohol, wealth or other luxuries, by self-sacrifice – flagellation, martyrdom, none of which were elements of traditional Judaism or the teachings of Jesus.

The law of the Torah, Talmud, etc. was designed to provide a firm basis on which Jews could practice not only an ethical life for themselves, but also a structure that would make the entire community run smoothly and avoid fights, vendettas or destructive confrontations not only among the Jews but in their dealings with others as well. It also required acts of charity, and a personal recognition of any wrongdoing with the requirement of atonement and corrective action. In many cases, while treated as if they were religious ordinances, they were often common sense rules of sanitation or hygiene, dress codes, ways of settling familial or marital discord or commercial disputes, inheritances, etc. These laws were usually well-known within a Jewish community and were read out throughout the year as part of the Torah reading during a weekly religious service. These laws also include the kosher laws and the necessity of circumcision. These latter two were the ways non-Jews identified and often belittled Jews since they seemed strange or unnecessarily ritualistic to them. Nonetheless, these laws were thought at the time to prevent serious health problems, such as venereal disease, salmonella, trichinosis.

The only deviation Jesus suggested was to make these laws actually more rigorous in one case, or more susceptible to rational application.

In the situation referred to above concerning the conflict between eating gathered grain on the Sabbath, Jesus is asking for a more human, reasonable application of the law rather than a rigid often irrational standard. But in another case, he seeks a somewhat deeper interpretation of the laws. He refers to the tenth commandment which says that a man should not covet his neighbor's wife, etc. Interestingly, this is the one commandment which does not proscribe an overt act – murder, theft, etc., but goes into the mind of the individual to prevent the act by forbidding the thought process in advance of the commission of a crime such as theft or adultery. Jesus expands on these by suggesting that merely looking at a woman means that he has "lust in his heart" as Jimmy Carter famously quoted. In this way, it seems that Jesus sought to go beyond obedience to a variety of known laws which could be objectively studied and rationally accepted and obeyed. Instead, he sought an internalization of these rules of right and wrong to have man police his own thoughts subjectively before he could form the intention to act.

In this way, Jesus tended to give the members of the community more leeway in making decisions. He was straying from the bounds of codified, time-tested hard and fast rules to a more liberal reasoning of moralistic behavior. In this, he may well have been influenced by Platonic teaching. In any event, he was clearly always working within the context of Jewish law and tradition, which Paul clearly rejected.

But Paul swept aside virtually all of the Torah, all the precedents created out of the Torah as well as the teachings of Jesus – which themselves were traditionally Jewish, but also in other ways unique to Jesus. Paul had created a series of moral views which he claimed came directly from his personal dreamlike encounter with Jesus, but were often a mixture of pagan mystery religions and personal moral judgments of an entirely unique nature.

Paul's instruction to the pagans that the Jewish law, or Torah, was not necessary for their salvation was a key element of his preaching. Not only does he refer disparagingly to circumcision and kosher laws, but he rejects knowledge of the law as an element in their salvation. Yet, in doing so, he sows in his letters the confusion and, often, chaos which ensued for the next 1,500 years. In 1Corinthians, he was asked a number of questions by the congregation and attempted to make responses guiding them. In doing so, he shockingly displays his own lack of knowledge of the law. He was being asked questions of the sort rabbis and priests, learned in the law, or ordinary congregants also learned, could address easily by reference to the Torah and the Talmud. Without referring to the law at all, he makes some impromptu responses.

In 1 Corinthians, Paul appeals to the lowest denominator in the group and abjures wisdom. "I will destroy the wisdom of the wise, the intelligence of the intelligent will I frustrate." 1Cor18. He deals with incest, lawsuits, sexual immorality, and married life, food sacrificed to idols – matter which one readily answered by the Torah and the law. Yet Paul does no research and uses no knowledge he might have learned in his years as a practicing Jew. He relies only on his own intuition, and his personal revelation of Jesus' death, resurrection and the imminence of his second coming. Unfortunately, this off-the-cuff memo of dealing with real life issues is open to prejudices, rationalizations, projections and a variety of defense mechanisms.

It was the abandonment of the Torah and the law as the anchor for a stable society with known legal standards that caused the drift in the definitions of morality. If the law is the bulwark of the poor and meek, its absence is an invitation to the incursion of the strong and self-willed. As a result, superior power and self-interest could fill the vacuum and subject the vast majority of the Christian world to serfdom. As a result, the oppressive Roman world was followed by a feudal system in which the church controlled the daily lives of the serfs and made the vast majority of the population of the western world essentially slaves to work the land for a few members of the nobility. The nexus of church and state created such ideas as the divine right of kings, and obedience and servility in the church-based codes of conduct.

Paul bore an extremely virulent antipathy to not only the main body of the Jews, but also the Jesus movement based in Jerusalem. In his letters, he makes almost no reference to the historical Jesus from the Gospels and no references to the Torah. He never refers to Jesus' own words or teachings. He relied solely on his own version of the resurrection and ascension into heaven as the Son of God, and insisted that faith in these beliefs was all that is essential to salvation, heaven or the afterlife, while good works or obedience to the law was not necessary.

What had sustained the Jews for over a thousand years, the written laws defined in the Torah was to be eliminated and replaced by divine revelation of those who believed they alone had the ability to communicate with Jesus directly. In order to understand the Torah and its precepts, Jews had to be a literate society and they were replaced by a society which did not require literacy as an essential element in religious life. Rather than basing their thinking on written principles of time-tested law, it permitted ad hoc reasoning or intuition to form moral judgements. As a result, what we know today as psychologic mechanisms were permitted free rein – such as rationalizations, paranoias, projections, denials, even schizophrenia could alter reality. It was as if boats had their rudders removed, and they were permitted to drift freely. Today, we often refer to our Judeo-Christian heritage as based on law and legal precedent. In reality, the Christian part of this tradition did not become part of our Western morality until after the English referred back to the Torah, began to read Hebrew and incorporated the Jewish tradition in the system of laws based on written laws and legal precedents and then became known as the Judeo-Christian tradition. Until then, the governance of a community was based on power – those with it made individualized decisions based on at best their own personal dictates or, at worst, expediency. For their daily lives the people looked to the village priest, who looked to the Church, subservient to the king and his vassals.

Paul then inserted a few doctrines entirely of his own creation. <u>Sola Vide</u> – the concept that salvation of the human spirit is achieved by <u>faith alone</u>, and not good works. The implications of this doctrine are far-reaching. What this doctrine does is to minimize if not do away with all ethical standards and replace them with decisions by those controlling the faithful. The "faith" portion requires a belief in Jesus. However, as it evolved beginning with Paul and proceeding down the centuries was a belief in the resurrection of Jesus in the three days following the crucifixion, his installation on the "right hand of God," his status as divine and his status as being a co-equal with God the Father. Jesus himself in many of his quoted statements never claimed to be divine. At best, he uses the term "Son of Man," – a generic term meaning essentially that he was humble and human. Rather, he seems to have believed that he was a human messiah inspired by God.

It is important to understand the environment in which Paul was attempting to get his message across. In the cities of Asia Minor, Greece and possibly Rome where Paul's travels took him, there were three different groups: the traditional Jews, the Jews who followed the Jesus movement and the non-Jews following various pagan religions.

As to the traditional Jews, they would have given Paul an extremely cold reception. Since they were already circumcised, any relief from this ritual was meaningless. They were all usually raised with some degree of Jewish education, many were literate and easily understood that as the "people of the book," they had a tradition of over 1,200 years of accumulated laws and commentary on laws in the Torah and Talmud and the ensuring books of the Haftarah. Portions of each were read and commented on regular basis every Sabbath during the year, and repeated every year thereafter. The Jewish communities were tight knit, and centered around the synagogue. Many Jews were engaged in trades or commerce which separated them from the local farmers or fishermen who made up the balance of the cities' population. To ask these traditional Jews to give up the Torah, the law or leave their communities would have required an extraordinary conversion under any circumstance.

A central point of Paul's claim was that Jesus was resurrected into heaven and was himself divine.

A vast portion of the Jews – especially mainstream Jews – never would have accepted the idea of a resurrection or an afterlife. Some Pharisees held a belief in resurrection but nothing on a par with what Paul preached. However, to call a man a god was entirely alien to any kind of Jewish belief. It would have been an utter blasphemy. It is no wonder that Paul was harmed physically and run out of numerous cities as was recounted in Acts, or in Paul's own letters.

Those Jews who became aligned with the Jesus movement in Jerusalem would quickly have seen through Paul's reasoning. A review of Paul's writings and Luke's Acts shows that Paul made almost no reference to the life of Jesus, or any of his parables or preaching as in the Gospels. Although the Gospels appear first in the New Testament, they were actually written well after the Acts or Paul's letters. Most of Jesus' teachings were totally ignored. Most importantly Jesus did not set out to form a religion – as he famously said "Think not that I am come to destroy the law, but to fulfill it." Jesus was a traditional mainstream Jewish preacher for the most part. He clashed frequently with the Pharisees on the observance of the ritual and the law, but never on its validity or place in the Jewish communities. For him to preach, as Paul claimed, that faith alone (Sola Vide) was necessary to achieve salvation and not good works would have contradicted everything Jesus believed. Many parables uphold the principle that people and even non-Jews who repent, or perform good acts, are held in high esteem while those who only perform ritual acts of piety are hypocrites.

Paul's only strong appeal was to those pagans. At the time, there were a number of what we call today pagan religions. In every area there was some pantheon of local gods who controlled various areas – fertility, family, the sun, the moon, war, etc. As the local people were conquered, the conquering culture would either insert forcibly or, simply by its overwhelming presence cause their own deities to be substituted for the local ones. Since the gods were often similar, the conquered people rarely resisted conversion. Only the Jews rebelled on religious principles. Since most of the local communities had a similar set of deities or had deities whose aspects wore a mixture of similar hats. Worship generally consisted of making a sacrifice, usually of an animal, making a prayer of praise to the god, and asking for something of value in return from the god. Since fertility, good harvest, good hunting, healthy flocks or herds, and many children were their main concerns, their gods were frequently asked to deliver on these prayers. Priests usually benefitted substantially from the process of sacrifice or offerings so the conquerors could erect their own temples and install their own priests. However, the religions rarely had a moral or ethical code, much less a written one. There was no sense that performing acts of goodness or kindness could be rewarded, or bad acts punished by the gods.

To these pagans, the full acceptance of the entire Jewish conversion ceremony would have been an enormous barrier. Circumcision was not a rite a grown male would be anxious to undergo. The kosher laws would have not been comfortable for pagans who were unfamiliar with them. These people were mostly illiterate. While they were comfortable with their own religions more often than not their gods did not appear to fulfill the requests in their prayers despite their sacrifices. Paul in effect postponed what adherence to religion promised until after death and promised a rich afterlife for those with more faith and not a resume of good deeds, or a moral life.

Paul's message was that Jesus was sent to earth by God, the Father, to take away the sins these pagans had committed. Accordingly, Jesus died a cruel and painful death by crucifixion to procure salvation for those who believed in him. Since all humans were sinners and Jesus was not, his death absorbed the prior sins and allowed those who believed in the resurrection to be reborn without sin. While life might be painful and difficult for many in this lifetime, those who believed in the divinity and resurrection of Jesus would receive a joyous reward in the afterlife. The pagans were then asked to believe Paul's personal and uncorroborated vision on the way to Damascus of his meeting with Jesus, and Paul's characterization of Jesus as the son of God, whose father caused him to suffer crucifixion in order to expiate all those who believed Paul's story.

Pagans were familiar with most of Paul's claims from their previous religious traditions. Almost all rulers claimed to be god, and demanded to be worshipped as such. Julius Caesar and Alexander the Great decreed they were gods among many others. The concept of divinity was not as exalted as that of the Jewish God. Resurrection was a concept they all were aware of, but this was mainly reserved for royalty for whom elaborate tombs were erected and furnished to serve them in a happy after life.

Peasant pagans were presumably not so lucky. So when Paul promised them a happy afterlife if they simply believed in the divinity of Jesus and his resurrection, they would receive the same benefit as the rulers and other wealthy people did. Since the divinity of a human ruler and the resurrections to an afterlife were concepts they were familiar with, the faith they were to ascribe to was all the unverifiable, revelations to Paul. However, it gave them hope and promised things which could not be verified. Unlike their prayers for fertility, rain, riches, power, good crops, large flocks or herds, the promise of eternal salvation and an afterlife could not be realized until after their death. By claiming descent from the patriarch Abraham, while bypassing the Torah, the books of Kings and Prophets, the entire Jewish law, and the teachings of the prophets, the pagan converts never were asked to accept a body of laws or precepts to govern their lives. As a result, Paul justified to his followers that power and superior military force could turn the vast majority of them into feudal serfs, or slaves while the mighty ruled by whim. But they were given an unverifiable promise that they would have a happy afterlife. Paul and his followers further believed that this afterlife was imminent and would occur during Paul's lifetime, so conversion was an urgent need and would be promptly rewarded.

Within the diasporan communities, scattered in the major cities of Asia Minor, around the Mediterranean, and even up the rivers of Europe, there were a number of synagogues who welcomed what were called "righteous gentiles." They had not converted to Judaism but wished to be included in the synagogue. For many years before Jesus, these non-Jews were welcomed but not held to all the 613 laws of the Torah, but were required to abide by the "Noahide Laws." These seven commandments were deemed to have originated with Noah – who was considered the common ancestor of all mankind since he was the survivor of the flood. Those surviving Noah who sought salvation while not Jewish – could by practicing under these laws be held compliant with God's dictates, and entitled to salvation. These laws, in simplified form were:

1. Do not deny God (a monotheistic God)

2. Do not curse or blaspheme God.

3. Do not murder.

4. Do not engage in incestuous, adulterous or homosexual relationships.

5. Do not steal (including any form of deceptive financial practice)

6. Do not eat an unclean animal (a reduced form of kosher diet)

7. Establish courts/legal system to ensure obedience to the law.

Number six was a variation on the extensive kosher laws, but the commandment prohibited eating butchered animals from whom the blood had not been drained as with standard kosher practices. The other kosher practices were not included such as mixing of dairy and meat dishes, the prohibited fish, birds or other animals, etc. Number five included a number of definitions including theft by fraud, force, etc.

Several principles arose from the Pauline version of Christianity that in some ways stunted the intellectual growth of the West during the dark ages. The Sola Vide Doctrine requiring only faith in Paul's theology without the necessity of good works allowed the Christian community to develop a powerful hierarchical feudal structure in which the "divine right of kings" made subordination to the feudal state a religious requirement enforced by the Church. Although perhaps unforeseen at the time, the requirement of unquestioning faith was co-opted by Constantine in the early fourth century, 325 CE, when he made the Christian religion the official religion of the Empire. While a gift of freedom and tolerance to the Christians, it also caused the Church to be remade into and subordinate to a Roman power with a standardized code of belief and a structure running from local priests up through bishops and on to Pope. With the village priest as confessor, the attendance at church in a state of grace to receive communion, the church was able to preserve and enforce feudal power structures as its companion. Not taking communion meant to the whole village that you were not confessing and therefore not in a state of grace.

By the Council of Nicaea in 325 BC, Constantine drew together some powerful members of the existing Christian community and had them standardize the religion's beliefs and declare the balance heresies. The natural consequence of this orthodoxy was persecution of the non-believers – Gnostics, and those who questioned the divinity of Jesus and others were persecuted more rigorously than the early Christians themselves – all with the considerable weight of the Roman Empire behind them.

As a result, the Pauline religion did away with the structure of Jewish law, and, by its absence, substituted Roman law. By eliminating literacy as a requirement of religious practice, he eliminated the need for literacy in daily affairs. By the doctrine of "Sola Vide," he made orthodoxy in religious matters without the necessity of good works, a basis for religious persecution and enabled Rome when it co-opted the orthodox religion, to use the religion as a weapon for state power.

It would be as if our entire Constitution, Bill of Rights, and all the laws and rulings by judges were swept away, and all rulings were made by a man who claimed to have a mystical relationship with a divine being. Until the Renaissance, Europe was unable to free itself from the full grip of the kings – who claimed to rule by divine right, and the Church hierarchy – who kept tight control of the peasant population.

The Church, with the Bible in Latin, restricted the interpretation of religious and social matters to the priesthood. The power of the confessional and the ability to receive communion in front of the town's populace were strong influences.

Paul AND SEX

RICHARD MALMED

In the early Christian movement, women often occupied positions of power and were frequently preachers especially in Gnostic communities. Sex per se in the Old Testament and the Jewish tradition over 12 centuries was not a sin, or a practice to be condemned. Paul without any prior precedent condemned both women and sex.

For some reason, only two religions appear to cast women in the role of potential seductresses and adulterers: Paul's pagan converts and Islam. In other religions, while women may not have been granted equal status with men, they are not viewed in such a threatening way. In India, women and sex are seen as gifts from the gods for pleasure and procreation. In China, women are viewed in much the same way but are accorded a role as commanders of the household, its servants and also the family business enterprise. In Judaism, the Song of Songs gives women a positive sexual role and, in Proverbs 31, a strong role in administering the family financial affairs. Paul's doctrine then appears to be the only religion at the time to have such a trepidation toward sex and women, which in many ways is similar to that of Islam.

Paul in Corinthians is quite forthright in his dislike of women, sex or marriage. As to celibacy, Paul wishes that all men "were as I (celibate)" Corinthians 7.6. Further, he says that "Those who marry will have an affliction in regard to the flesh (7.28) and I would spare you that. (7.38) It is well for a man not to touch a woman. (7.1) and it is better to marry than to burn. (7.9)" Whether Paul was expressing his own personal aversion to sex and women, or raising the concept to a theological injunction is unclear. Never before had sexual abstention been asserted as a universal religious principle. Different sects including the Essenes practiced celibacy for periods of time as a form of personal religious sacrifice similar to fasting, but never as a lifetime mandate.

It is difficult to see where the concept that birth control or masturbation became issues in theology. Until Thomas Malthus' famous work on population, there was always biblical directive to be fruitful and multiply. Sex then was a pleasant catalyst to support this divine exhortation. Large families were seen as signs of prosperity and encouraged. The harmless, victimless act of masturbation was not singled out for any comment anywhere.

After Malthus, the limitation on population growth was seen as a positive concept for the modern era. Birth control was the fortuitous answer to human sexual desire and excessive population density. There was no logical basis for a denial of either.

The Jews felt that sex was a gift from God to be enjoyed but not abused. To read the Song of Songs is to understand the Jewish attitude toward sex. It was supposedly written by King Solomon over 1,000 years before Paul and venerated over the centuries by Jews. Solomon had over 700 wives and 300 concubines. David also had many wives and concubines. Jews even had a little known practice of holy prostitutes known as "kedushah". Sex was considered one of God's blessings.

There were a number of prohibitions, however, in the pursuit of sex. Incest was clearly defined within certain degrees of relationship. Although this may seem dangerous today in light of our knowledge of genetics, most pagans of the time and especially the ruling families were encouraged to practice incest if they did not marry the neighboring potentate's daughters for diplomatic reasons. Adultery was essentially a sin against the contract of marriage. A man having sexual relations with another man's wife was causing a breach of the marital contract which would usually lead to blood feuds and vendettas. Fornication, per se, was not a sin if no other law was breached. While virginity was prized, a woman who was not a virgin was simply a poor marital bargain and might not attract a suitable husband.

Although Paul's fear of sex or dislike of women does not seem to have taken hold within the early Christian communities, his influence is strongly felt over the later periods. Men are encouraged to abstain, and Church officials are required to be celibate. Women are forbidden to become preachers and, when they did join the Church, had limited roles as housekeepers, educators of early childhood and farm hands.

Admittedly, in Jewish practice, women were relegated to positions behind screens on the second floor during religious services. Similarly, they could neither become bar mitzvah or become ordained as rabbis. Yet they were expected to hold very important roles in the family business and as helpmates to their husbands. (See Proverbs 31).

However, Jesus himself and his disciples never encouraged the practice of abstinence or celibacy. One exception appears to be the Essenes who had a ritualized form of marriage which limited sexual activity. Also, excepting the Essenes, the Jews never believed in self-sacrifice, or self-punishment, or self-denial and were encouraged to view life as a gift even if at times it could be painful or difficult.

There is no support for any of Paul's attitudes towards women or sex in any of Jesus' teachings. There is no evidence that Jesus was not married, or practiced celibacy or abstinence. His relationship with Mary Magdalene was unusually close (See Gospel of Mary). A Jewish man in his 30s who was not married would have been viewed with suspicion. Since the fact of his marital or sexual relations or lack thereof is not mentioned in the Gospels, it suggests that there may have been a relationship that made him appear to have human qualities which might diminish his image of being pure or godlike. Certainly, if he had a female companion, it would not have been a harmful aspect to his image among Jews. It is significant that Jesus was depicted as preventing the stoning of a woman held in adultery by telling only those without sin to cast the first stone. In this way, he was able to demonstrate his antipathy to hypocrisy but also showed he was soft on strict punishment for a sexual crime. David, Solomon, Moses and many others had healthy sexual relationships often with more than their wives and demonstrated great respect for women in their narratives. Esther, Bathsheba, the Queen of Sheba, and Zipporah, all exercised strong influences on men and were strong women respected for their beauty as well as their opinions. Paul's apparent personal aversion to women and sex has been transmitted as Church doctrine for the past 2,000 years. While sex and relationships among the sexes can be complicated, it has been detrimental to western civilization to have the awesome power of the church disseminating guilt for the practice of sex in the appropriate context. It has undoubtedly lead to inhibitions in women, and made the marital relationship more difficult, yet there appears to be no basis in the Jewish Bible or in Jesus' sayings for sexual repression.

Barabbas

RICHARD MALMED

Something should be said about the references to Barabbas in the various Gospels. First there is no known tradition that permitted the release from crucifixion of a convicted person by either the Romans or the Jews. It has the sound of a pagan tradition in which a sacrificial animal was released. It also has the sound of a literary device to demonstrate the evil of the Jews who would vote to release a convicted thief in lieu of Jesus who, whether you believe him to be divine or a pious holy man, certainly deserved to be exonerated of his charges more than a thief. But the very story betrays some interesting points of view.

The very name Barabbas is itself a signal that the story's author knew no Hebrew or Aramaic, and even less of Jewish culture. As such, he would certainly be entitled to no credibility as a historian. This use of such a name as if it were the given name of an actual person clearly shows it was an invention by a pagan from Asia Minor or Greece. The actual name would be Bar Abbas, meaning, to any Jew or even someone from the surrounding areas "the son of the father." "Bar" a widely recognized Semitic term for "son of " and "abbas" meaning father. No one would have been so named in the Semitic culture. It was probably a chosen "nom de guerre" or a nickname chosen by a guerilla warrior to conceal his true identity.

Further, the Romans referred to these guerillas as "Laestes" which often means thief or bandit. It was a term of contempt used by the Romans because they considered members of these groups to be troublemakers or, in actual fact, terrorists. However, the use of the term suggests that they were in it for the money rather than as selfless patriots. It certainly was a Roman or Greek term and not one a contemporary Aramaic-speaking Jew would have used.

Jesus may have been crucified between two guerilla warriors, but this is unlikely. Joseph of Arimathea had somehow persuaded Pilate to permit the crucifixion to occur on land he owned near his family's burial cave, and not along the main road so that the body might be viewed as a warning to others considering the same act. The body would deteriorate and be attacked by scavenger birds over several days to further humiliate the victim even in death.

It is even more curious that Pilate would permit Jesus' body to be made available for burial by Joseph a mere six hours after being put on the cross. Thus, it is a colossal mystery that the body disappeared three days later and its disappearance was discovered by Mary Magdalene – a relative of Arimathea's and Lazarus' as well as possibly being Jesus' lover or wife or a close personal confidant.

The exoneration of "Barabbas" then by Pilate must be considered a fiction to bolster the idea that the Jews sought Jesus' crucifixion and not the Romans.

NEXT CHAPTER

THE CRUCIFIXION

The CRUCIFIXION

RICHARD MALMED

The crucifixion narrative in the gospels and other traditions present far more questions than answers.

In most of the depictions of the crucifixion, Jesus is shown with nails piercing the palms of his hands. Experiments by a Dr. Barbet[1] in 1937, have substantially disproven this theory. Assuming Jesus weighed about 160 pounds, it might be assumed that his weight was evenly distributed between the two hands. However, with each arm extending at a 68 degree angle, the force on each palm was measured at 209 pounds each. Barbet's experiment with freshly amputated hands disclosed that a force of only 88 pounds was sufficient to rip through the tendons, skin and even bones of the hands. It should be noted that those being crucified were known to pull up on their hands to relieve the asphyxiation they were then experiencing caused further stress.

The next plausible location for any nails would have been in the area on the wrist known as Destot's Space – between the capitate semilunar, triquetral and hamate bones of the wrist or the little finger (ulnar side) of the hand. This theory contradicts any suggestion that the Shroud of Turin is a legitimate relic from the crucifixion because the wound appears on the thumb (radial) side of the wrist.

Suggestions that the nails were driven through various points of parts of the wrist must be eliminated because they raise the highly probably result that Jesus would have suffered from lethal exsanguination (bleeding out) within a very short period after being placed on the cross. In other words, the highly likely prospect that either nail would have pierced a major artery in the wrist area would have caused Jesus to have bled out within 10 minutes to an hour. The extreme blood loss by itself would have caused large flows in the back and the front of the upper area of both wrists to have caused death well short of the six hour timeframe allotted for his remaining life. It should be noted that the Shroud of Turin shows little blood around the palm or wrist despite the presence of many arteries and veins in the area.

While the lack of any nails to the palms or wrists may cause the disbelief in many mythical depictions of the crucifixion, including the Shroud of Turin, it is far more likely that Jesus was tied to the patibulum (the cross piece) and that it was intended that he die of asphyxiation.

---

1   P. Barbet, Le Cinge Plaies due Christ, 2d Ed (1937)

The first and most intriguing question is who was Joseph of Arimathea. His name is a unique combination. It is impossible to resist being drawn to the "thea" as the end of his name. Most people with a surname or designation used either the name of a place or the name of their father or tribe. Only Luke stated that Arimathea was a city in Judea. No other gospel, scholar or other source recognizes this location to having ever been in existence. If somehow the name was a combination of Greek and Hebrew, the "thea" is a Greek word for God, and the "ha ram" or "ha rama" refers to the top. The name could be interpreted to be "the highest of God."

We also know that Joseph was an "honourable counselour" who sat on the Sanhedrin but was also either an overt or a secret (Mark 15:43) follower of Jesus. The family of Mary Magdalene and Lazarus certainly knew him well or may have been related to him.

Next, and most important, although a Jew and even an overt member of the Sanhedrin, Joseph had considerable influence with Pontius Pilate. In some cases, these influences led to serious breaches of security by the Roman soldiers at the crucifixion and at the tomb.

If the crucifixion had followed the accepted Roman formula, Jesus would have been put on the cross along a major highway where he could linger in painful death throes for several days until he died in public view so as to intimidate others fostering revolutionary ideas. Then, his body would slowly rot while his eyes were pecked out by birds. Eventually, he would be placed in a common burial pit to be forgotten. A combination of deviations from this plot was negotiated by Joseph of Arimathea with Pontius Pilate which created a series of events which lead one of the most startling of historical events – the disappearance of Jesus' body from the tomb by Monday. These factual additions tend to be more credible because they do not support the anti-Semitic theme as other agendas of most in the gospels but seem to add only gratuitous forensic evidence to the narrative.

1. Pilate permitted the crucifixion to occur in Joseph of Arimathea's private garden – Golgotha.

2. Jesus was administered an unknown and uninspected substance by sponge and, by all outward appearances, died immediately

after only six hours on the cross.

3. Joseph of Arimathea and Nicodemus are permitted to take the body down and place it in his family tomb adjacent to his private garden.

4. Lazarus, a close friend of Jesus, was apparently brought forth from the dead after three days in a startlingly similar parallel to that of Jesus.

5. Jesus' body disappeared three days after his apparent death.

6. No Roman soldier was present when the stone covering the front of the tomb was removed and Mary Magdalene discovered Jesus' body had disappeared.

Joseph prevailed on Pilate to permit the crucifixion to occur in Golgotha – a "garden" outside of the city walls that Joseph's family owns. He secured the command to have Jesus declared dead and taken to Joseph's own burial cave. Joseph and Nicodemus both members of the Sanhedrin themselves actually took Jesus down from the cross. Joseph of Arimathea's tremendous use of clout raises the doubt that the other irregularities of the crucifixion process were not mere coincidences, but must have been part of a plot of Joseph's making.

A major forensic issue arises from the length of time Jesus was on the cross. We know that those Jews who received Jesus after his arrest in the Garden of Gethsemane around midnight turned him over to the Romans early the next morning. Then Pilate himself either tried Jesus, or sent him to Herod Antipas for trial. If so, Antipas returned him promptly following his refusal to exercise jurisdiction. In either case, Jesus must have been condemned to crucifixion as early as about 9:00 a.m. We know he died at the "sixth hour" or about 3:00 p.m. Six hours on the cross was an exceedingly short time to linger on the cross before death. Most of those crucified lasted several days on the cross before death ensued. Jesus lasted only six hours before he was declared dead. It is suggested that someone administered either a poison or a drug to cause the appearance of death to relieve Jesus of the incredible pain he was suffering, rather than let him pass out and lessen the agony. What is significant, if it was a member of his entourage at the cross who administered it, is that there might have been a coma or death-inducing substance that was on the sponge. At that time, there were many concoctions known to induce a deathlike or coma-like state. The term "gall" as the potion is described in Matthew 27:3 could well have been an extract of mandrake root which had those qualities or some opiate. It is even more significant that Lazarus entered into the same coma-like trance a year earlier and those in Bethany thought him dead. Lazarus was a much beloved friend of Jesus and probably a cousin or brother of Mary Magdalene. When Jesus was told first of his illness, he curiously delayed two days before making the journey to heal Lazarus John 11:1-45. When Jesus arrived, he was told he was too late and that Lazarus had died. Nonetheless, Jesus without ceremony, prayer or any other ritual activity simply ordered Lazarus to rise from his tomb which he then did. The Lazarus incident is so close in time to Jesus' crucifixion as to suggest it may have been a dress rehearsal for Jesus, if he indeed regained consciousness after being taken down from the cross.

It is curious that Jesus' body even if dead was removed from the cross so early. Normally, bodies rotted and deteriorated for several days on a public highway where they could terrorize those in the public who contemplated similar acts. Pilate may have been persuaded that he wished to avoid such a display during Passover. On the other hand, Joseph of Arimathea may have negotiated it.

There is certainly something more going on here than meets the eye. A number of theories are possible. 1) Joseph of Arimathea negotiated Jesus' escape on the promise that Jesus leave Jerusalem and avoid anti-Roman activity, 2) Joseph negotiated a sufficient number of security breaches with Pilate that a) Simon of Cyrene or someone else substituted for Jesus, b) Jesus could be removed from the cross before he was dead and, while in a chemically induced state appearing to be like death, and was revived later in Joseph's tomb, without Pilate's knowledge or consent.

Some other facts support these theories. The Roman guards never broke Jesus' legs. This would normally have been considered an act of kindness to hasten death or to relieve the guards of extra work. However, if Jesus survived the crucifixion, he would not have to suffer broken legs.

It is also of interest that the Quran states that Jesus was not crucified. Quran 4:157-158.

It is no less curious that Jesus was taken down from the cross but then placed in the friendly confines of Joseph's family tomb where under normal circumstances his body would have been permitted to deteriorate for a year when the flesh would have rotted off the bones which would then be placed in an ossuary or bone box. If Jesus were simply unconscious at this point he would wake up in an area under Joseph's control rather than a common burial pit. Normally, his body would simply rot on the cross until it was removed and placed in a common resting place. The body being confined to areas under Joseph's control prevented the inquiry of nosy third parties in the post-crucifixion events. It is significant that the gospels claim that there were guards posted at the tomb, but that there were no guards present when Mary discovered the empty tomb, or when the stone was rolled aside.

After three days in the tomb, Jesus' body disappeared. After four days, Lazarus also rose from being apparently dead – a parallelism too difficult to ignore.

Mary Magdalene and possibly other women, came to the tomb on the third day and discovered the large stone covering the tomb had been rolled aside. At the time of her "discovery," there was no Roman soldier guarding the tomb. In several of the gospels, men dressed in white were in the vicinity of the tomb. Essenes were known for their wearing of white clothes. It is well known that Jesus espoused a number of Essene doctrines, including the apocalyptic view that if the Jews repented their sins and returned to lives of piety, God would usher in a world of peace and justice although he never accepted their monastic lifestyle. It could well be that these men in white were Essenes. These men in white could well have been yet another complication to the Jesus' story which tantalizes us with tidbits of evidence for no apparent political motive that fits the gospel writers' anti-Semitic agendas.

It is possible to resist the notion that these gratuitous and curious elements in the gospels point to a very unorthodox interpretation of the crucifixion narrative. It is certainly possible to speculate that Jesus did not die on the cross, but was given a potion creating a temporary coma-like appearance from which Jesus recovered in the family tomb of Joseph of Arimathea and was spirited away by friendly accomplices, possibly Essene priests.

On the other hand, Jesus may have been poisoned to death in the sixth hour to hasten his death and shorten his suffering. In either case, it would militate against the theory of resurrection on which so much of Paul's doctrine and, as a result, a large portion of Christianity depend. While it may do so, it is not the intent of this analysis to shake the faith of many good Christians. In fact, quite the opposite. It may be that much of the Christian faith is weighed down with too much theology, mythology or required beliefs that Jesus' personal message may be lost in the process. Certainly, vicious wars were fought in Europe in the Hundred Years War, the Crusades, and many, many other destructive confrontations to impose by force one or more doctrinal issues on others. The concept of sole fida or "only faith" is one which Paul, Martin Luther and many Christian thinkers since have asserted as the primary basis for associations with the Christian Church. It requires a belief in the resurrection of Jesus, the divinity of Jesus, and the nature of the trinity as the sole basis for salvation to the exclusion of all those who do not accept any portion of those beliefs. Good works, or repentance for past sins are essentially irrelevant under the doctrine of sole fida. Belief in any other religion disqualifies the believer from salvation. As a corollary, the death of Jesus, and often the acts or the martyrdom of the saints also removes sins from a true believer without any positive act of atonement or love on his or her part.

A close scrutiny of the facts concerning the crucifixion may lead to a more positive acceptance by the individual for his own acts, rather than the reliance on Jesus or the saints, and lead to more tolerance, and affirmative acts of social welfare. It may result also in closer attention to Jesus' own legitimate message.

NEXT
CHAPTER

SANHEDRIN TRIAL

Sanhedrin TRIAL

RICHARD MALMED

The issue of what happened at the Sanhedrin trial following the Passover meal of Jesus and his disciples has been a piece of history that has engendered devastating repercussions over the last 2,000 years. The gospel's version of what occurred is simply not supported by the facts of Jewish law, a comparison of the gospels, or any reasonable forensic analysis. As per the Gospels, Jesus and his entourage held a Passover eve meal in Jerusalem and then retired to the slopes of Gethsemane, a walk of about 30 to 45 minutes from Jerusalem. During the meal, Jesus revealed that one of the disciples would "betray" him, at which point, Jesus told Judas to do what must be done. Judas then left presumably to betray Jesus by leading members of the guard from the Jewish Temple to arrest him. Judas later identified Jesus by giving him a kiss and the guard forthwith arrested him and brought him not to the Sanhedrin chambers but to the house of Ananas the father-in-law of the then high priest Caiaphas. This would have been about midnight. Then between 12:00 a.m. and the early morning hours of Passover day, the Sanhedrin – the high deliberative body of the Jews – found Jesus guilty of blasphemy and, in the hours around dawn of that day, turned Jesus over to the Romans for execution. Pontius Pilate, the Roman prosecutor then, made many attempts to avoid Jesus' execution by first sending Jesus to Herod Antipas, then when Antipas refused to try him, Pilate several times thereafter tried to avoid executing him. A careful analysis of the widely accepted facts demonstrates this version to be false.

It should be remembered that the authors of the gospels had a strong political agenda to avoid blaming Rome for Jesus' death and shifting the blame to the Jews of Jerusalem. The key fact here is that there was a violent and nearly successful uprising by the Jews between 67 and 70 CE, after which the Temple was destroyed and the power and prestige of the Jewish followers of Jesus in Jerusalem virtually extinguished. It should also be noted that Sadducees had James, Jesus' brother, killed in the absence of the Roman procurator about 62 CE. It should also be noted that there was an ongoing dispute between the traditional Jews and James the Just, the brother of Jesus, who had assumed a leadership role in the Jesus Movement in Jerusalem. Ananas who was then high priest in Jerusalem, in the absence of a Roman procurator, had James stoned to death in 62 CE. From that point forward, the followers of

Paul in Asia Minor were left to tell and interpret their version of the story of Jesus. These men were often not raised in the Jewish tradition, or had any prior allegiance to Jerusalem. In fact, at the behest of Paul, they were frequently told to ignore the "Law" which meant the study of the Torah and the compilation of legal thought built up over the previous 1,000 years but to rely solely on faith ("Sole Vida") for making moral decisions and guiding their daily lives.

Although in the Gospels the actual arrest was effected by varying groups of people, sometimes they are designated simply as Temple guard, sometimes as "a multitude," and sometimes "priests or scribes" are included. Modern historians agree that there was a "cohort" or a speira of Roman soldiers who accompanied the Temple guard, John 19. A cohort would have been between about 500 Roman soldiers. The undoubted presence of a such a large Roman presence must be seen as Pilate's having a strong interest in the removal of Jesus as a possible threat to security.

On the other hand, the presence of "priests," "scribes" or "elders" as are sometimes referred to is highly unlikely. If the event took place on the hours following Passover eve, or the evening of Passover day, the priests certainly would have been overwhelmed with their duties administering to the sacrifices at the Temple and their functions during the rites of Passover. Jerusalem had swelled from 25,000 to 250,000 with pilgrims – almost all of whom needed to have animals sacrificed during that weekend. The priests never would have taken the time off to deal with a matter best left to trained policemen or soldiers.

By the scribes and elders, the gospels may be either referring to actual members of the Sanhedrin or other highly ranked people in the Jerusalem community. Their presence during a 45 minute trek from the city to Gethsemane across the Kidron Valley and back to make an arrest is unlikely. They would most certainly have been home with their families who, like Jesus and his disciples, had participated earlier in the Passover service and meal. It is inconceivable that they would have left their homes to show solidarity with the Temple guard and a Roman cohort to effect an arrest, when they were not needed.

Even more to the point, the arrest was intentionally staged at Gethsemane at an hour and a place when a large number of contingent

– whether onlookers, supporters or protestors – would assuredly be an impediment to the public arrest of a popular preacher.

While there may have been elements in the Jewish community in Jerusalem that did not favor Jesus, there certainly were at least sufficient numbers that did. It is more likely that there were much greater support among the pilgrims than the contrary position.

At least, then it is possible to say from the facts of the arrest that Pilate's interest was joined with certain elements in the Jewish hierarchy that wanted Jesus dealt with. The arrest was a joint effort, coordinated in advance, and designed to take place with as few of Jesus' followers present as possible. A remote location and an obscure hour were purposely chosen.

Now begins the analysis of just what the Sanhedrin did or did not do. The Sanhedrin court for capital offenses consisted of 23 prominent members of the Jewish community and included Sadducees – the wealthy hereditary priesthood that controlled Temple affairs, the Pharisees – men who conducted religious training, services, and performed other religious functions in the towns outside Jerusalem, and the scribes – well respected lay people. Each group had its own political position on the court and in Jewish life, and each was particularly protective of its prerogatives in that regard. The Sadducees while holding hereditary positions, and deriving great wealth from their sacerdotal functions – including in particular the Passover sacrifices at the Temple were nonetheless beholden to Rome. As was Roman policy, they permitted the local priests, courts and other day to day functions in the lives of the conquered peoples to remain the same as prior to their takeover. However, the Romans controlled the office of high priest and, in fact, kept his robes under lock and key to be released only for appropriate functions. To some degree, the Sadducees may be viewed as collaborators with Rome.

For that reason, the Sadducees were neither liked nor trusted by the common people who only grudgingly paid a Temple tax on top of Roman taxes to support this wealthy group. It is absurd to believe that they could have drawn a following of common people in support of their political agenda.

The Pharisees were a group of religious men whose calling was to enforce an extreme form of observance of Jewish laws and customs. Overly strict rules for items such as hand washing procedures, Sabbath observance, and other daily functions were challenged at every occasion. They for the most part acted as local holy men in the towns throughout the Jewish world outside of Jerusalem. They served an important role in teaching and preserving Jewish institutions. Jesus had a number of disputes with them concerning their excessive interpretation of religious law and rules. However, religious disputes over laws and observances was always part of the Jewish tradition. A negative opinion or even a criminal indictment could not arise out of a doctrinal debate.

The scribes' political or religious positions would vary according to where they came from and what their business was.

Since all three groups were represented on the Sanhedrin, the evidence would have to be very strong to obtain a joint guilty verdict.

It should also be understood that the Jews were known as the people of the book or the law. That means that from the time of Moses, the Jews had attempted to develop a series of written and oral laws over the 1,000 years prior to Jesus' arrest. Learned scribes had started codifying them in written form during and after the Babylonian exile (600s BCE) and over the centuries rabbis had commented and debated the nuances of the laws in oral form which were later recorded in the Talmud, the Mishnah and the Gemmorah.

So when Jesus was brought into the palace of the high priest's father-in-law Ananas for some type of action, there was a 1,000 year old tradition governing criminal law and procedure. A review of the many irregularities in procedure alone makes the existence of any trial to be totally incomprehensible. Whatever remedies enemies of Jesus sought to exact by this proceeding would have been null and void. It is obvious from the very simple facts in the gospels that the Jewish organization could never have even attempted to find guilt or seek the death penalty from Rome as has been recorded in the gospels at this early morning proceeding.

First, the site for conducting a hearing of the Sanhedrin was specified in the Torah to be one of three places. The gospels unswervingly contend that the trial took place at the palace of the high priest's father-in-law Ananas. (Deut 17:8-10). That place could never have been the venue for a trial.

Second: Cases were to be tried only during the day, never at night. (M Sanhedrin IV from the Mishna) Similarly, no one was to be tried on the eve of a Sabbath or festival day.

Third: No person was to be convicted on his own testimony (Deut 17:6). Instead, two separate witnesses must present uncontradicted, competent evidence against the accused. Deut 19:15 T Sanhedrin XI. In fact, confessions were not admissible at all in a capital case. The rational being that a man could not by incriminating himself, indirectly commit suicide.

Fourth: No person accused of a capital offense may be put to death other than after a conviction of a court of twenty-three based on the strength of two competent witnesses not only as to the commission of the offense, but also as to the fact that the offender was warned beforehand that if he committed the offense he would incur the death penalty. The two witnesses had to be direct eyewitnesses, and in all respects, under cross-examination, fully corroborate each other.

The fact that these well-known points of Jewish law were ignored in the gospel narrative suggests that the writers had no background at all in the Torah and were raised as pagans. It should be recalled that the entire Torah was read out to each congregation during the course of a year. The average adult would have heard these rules mostly from Deuteronomy at least 10 to 15 times by the time he was 25. Certainly, everyone in the Sanhedrin would have thoroughly known the criminal procedure.

It should be remembered that Jews were known as "people of the book" meaning they were educated in and expected to observe diligently the laws in the book – the Torah. In case the Sadducees might wish to slide by, the Pharisees, whose punctilious insistence on exaggerated and ritualized daily practices such as fasting, preparing food, washing hands, bathing, would never have put a man to death on less than a full and complete procedure in full compliance with the Torah. An irregularity at trial by the judges would have been harshly dealt with.

We have many other irregularities as well. Somehow, the chief priest Caiaphas was permitted not only to sit in judgement of Jesus, but as his chief and sole prosecutor. Such a deviation in jurisprudence where the prosecutorial function is merged with the judicial one is a blatant irregularity. In a similar and more obvious deviation, Jesus was struck by one of the guards during the cross-examination by Caiaphas in order to elicit a confession. Jewish law also permitted Jesus to be represented by a lawyer. None was offered, and he was not provided with enough time to get one.

Another interesting aspect in the list of errors is that the Sadducees should have recused themselves for sitting as judges; They should have removed themselves from those sitting in judgment. The law was clear that judges should avoid accepting bribes. In the reasoning on this issue, indirect financial benefit from a verdict was considered to be an attenuated form of bribe. To question Jesus on the issue of his challenging the moneychangers in the Temple was tantamount to attempting to interfere with this source of livelihood for the Sadducees.

The composition of this tribunal is further in doubt. With the trial scheduled on such short notice, at such an inconvenient (and illegal time) and in such a possibly hostile environment, it is probable that the requisite number of members was not available. Surely, those elements among the scribes or Pharisees who were not represented would have objected fiercely to any proceeding which did not contain their political colleagues. Many scribes and Pharisees might and probably did live a distance from Jerusalem and did not make the trek there this particular year. The legal issue of notice as well as the factual absence of many Sanhedrin members would have rendered any attempt at a trial to be a meaningless effort.

It should be presumed that, in a matter such as this, the entire Sanhedrin court of 23 members should be present. Yet there is still a requirement that the entire membership of either body was notified in proper time and was appropriately represented. This brings forward the next issue. We know further that Joseph of Arimathea, a prominent scribe and Nicodemus, a prominent Pharisee, were followers and supporters of Jesus, it is hard to see how they would vote for guilt.

The gospels do not indicate that Jesus was ever told of or was charged with a particular crime. While the Romans may have had an agenda based on acts of sedition, the Jews had to be confined only to the charge of blasphemy, which was punishable by death. Blasphemy as defined, was saying or writing the actual name of God. At no time was Jesus ever considered to have done so. He certainly embarrassed the Sadducees with his action in the Temple against the money changers but this was not a capital offense. It may have involved civil disturbance or damage to property but not an offense punishable by death. Jesus may have predicted he could destroy the Temple in three days, it was not a capital offense and should have been seen as one of his many metaphors. It has been written (in Mark) that Jesus claimed to be the Son of God. None of the other gospel writers support this observation, nor do any witnesses appear to have come forward to attest to it. Further, the reference to "Son of God" or often "Son of Man" was a colloquial term of art to indicate the person was human and a believer in God. It should never have been construed to imply that Jesus was claiming to be divine.

While in the Roman, Greek and other pagan religions, certain humans including especially rulers such as Julius Caesar or Alexander the Great might be worshipped as divine, this would never have been a Jewish concept. Pagan gods were free to seduce women, cheat and lie, overindulge in wine, and more particularly impregnate human women, Jews never could conceive of their God doing any such thing. Jesus was in his preaching essentially Jewish as were almost all of his followers. Only the pagans of Asia Minor converted by Paul could have conceived as someone with human flesh being at the same time divine. The Jewish God has no form or physical substance and while he could be heard, was never seen.

Instead, it is suggested that there never was a trial, and that the claim that the scribes and Pharisees were in attendance is wholly false. It seems that Jesus was merely interrogated in front of some Sadducees, who knew that they could not alone pronounce a sentence or even conduct a trial because of the many defects cited above. Rather, they were aware Jesus had become a major irritant and threatened to interfere with the Sadducees comfortable position by disrupting the sacrifice ritual. By drawing many coreligionists to him and preaching, while an essentially Jewish doctrine, it conflicted in practice occasionally with those of the Pharisees. Thus, he may have been asked "if he claimed either to be the King of the Jews or the Messiah." If he had answered yes to either of these, he still would not have committed a capital offense.

The concept of a messiah was a general term. It implied that the person was neither a military man nor a prophet, a king or some other function. David, as king, certainly saved the Jews from a Philistine threat as a military man. Throughout biblical history, men such as Eli, or Nathan were holy men, who while holding little power, elected or anointed other men as kings. Others were prophets who urged the people to abandon wicked or ungodly ways in order to save the nation. It would not have been a capital offense to claim to be a messiah, nor would it mean he should be prosecuted. If he turned out to be a messiah, fine. If he was not, history would deal with him. Jesus appears to have aspired only to be a preacher to the nation of Jews, and have them adopt principles of love, charity, good works, atonement and adoration of God. None of these ideas was either non-Jewish or criminal.

One version of events was that the Sanhedrin could not sentence Jesus to death even if they convicted him of a capital crime, but required Pilate and the Romans to execute him after they had their own trial. This premise is not true. The Sanhedrin did have the power and in fact did pronounce guilty verdicts in capital cases and order executions. Their methods of execution were strictly limited to stoning or burning, but the crucifix was specifically not permitted. If the Sanhedrin wished to execute Jesus and knew that, by sending him to Pilate, he would be crucified, they were acting contrary to Jewish law which proscribed crucifixion. In this case, they would have indirectly been violating their own law with full knowledge of the consequences.

In short, the gospel's version that "a trial" occurred must be wholly rejected. The implication that Jesus was forwarded to Pilate for execution must also be rejected. Pilate must be seen to have acted solely on his own and in consideration solely of Rome's interest in avoiding possible revolutionary elements during Passover.

NEXT CHAPTER

JEWISH MYTHS

Jewish MYTHS

RICHARD MALMED

There are two significant Jewish myths that have had harmful effects on Jewish development over the centuries. The first is the interpretation of the first and second commandments. The second is the kosher laws and other similar restrictions on contacts with non-Jews. The commandments have always been considered the word of God directly handed down to Moses. The kosher laws were largely man-made laws designed for governing the Jewish community.

First and Second Commandments

As originally transcribed, the laws governing the worshipping of other gods and the worshipping of idols were divided into two distinct commandments. The first dealt only with the reference to other gods, the second dealt with idols. The Catholic version of these commandments eliminated the second commandment entirely, but changed the tenth commandment governing the act of coveting into two parts – one as to "thy neighbor's wife," the other as to "thy neighbor's goods." Thus, the Jewish version of the Ten Commandments is substantially different from that of the Catholics.

The denial of the use of idols was an extremely progressive factor in the development of Judaism and western civilization in general. Credited to Abraham, whose father was ironically an idol maker, the concept of monotheism and the rejection of idol worship was a major advance in the western world's ethos. Pagans who worshiped many idols were essentially pursuing a lifestyle which was based on nature, and divided nature into many different aspects which were represented by material objects. This had many adverse consequences. If, for example, your wife was barren and you sought relief from a god of fertility, you sacrificed to that deity and expected something in return. If that didn't happen, you perhaps sought help from other deities on a quid pro quo basis. There was no expectation that by acting in a moral way or adhering to a moral code you would obtain the object you sought. Since the particular god only ruled fertility, or perhaps the wind, the sun, the water, the sea, etc., its jurisdiction was limited and it was only moved by material sacrifices.

On the other hand, a monotheistic God was universal in nature, and expected moral acts, or acts which supported the community over which God was the protector.

Idol worship further took away any responsibility for the acts of the individual seeking his attention. The supplicant to an idol could lead whatever life he wished and engage in murder, theft, adultery or any other amoral or antisocial acts he wished and still receive the benefit of his sacrifice.

By banning the practice of idol worship, the religious ethos placed directly on the individual the responsibility for obedience to God, the moral code and the importance of his relationship to the community in which he lived.

While quite laudatory in its initial purpose, the tendency of Jewish leaders, rabbis, scholars over the years has been to expand the import of these precepts to illogical conclusions. In the New Testament, Jesus points up the excessive reliance on ritual behavior when he confronted the Pharisees – a religious faction at the time that insisted on punctilious observance of the law. Jesus' men had had a particular long and hard day, and, on the Sabbath, went into a field to glean the fallen grain for their meal. These men and Jesus were scolded by the Pharisees for violating the commandment. Jesus responded that the law was made for men, i.e. that it should be interpreted liberally and in accordance with the situation at hand and not formalistically. He used the example of an ox fallen into a ditch on the Sabbath. Clearly, it would be better to save the ox than to have it die needlessly in order to avoid physical work on the Sabbath. Math 12:1, 11.

Unfortunately, Judaism has exaggerated the interpretation of the commandment concerning idols to include depictions of any and all men in any form of visual art, two or three dimensional. As a result, there has been virtually no Jewish art prior to the nineteenth century except for animals, agriculture or inanimate objects. From the explosion of art by Jewish artists thereafter, it is clear that such a deprivation was a major loss to western civilization and the communication of Jewish culture to it. Western and Jewish culture was denied artists that might have had the talents of Camille Pisarro, Amodeo Modigliani, Chaim Soutine, Jacques Lipchitz among others. Although the Catholic Church had some violent disputes in the eighth and ninth centuries in which some members of the clergy sought to ban icons and other human depictions, they eventually lost out. While the Catholics were enjoying the gothic, renaissance, baroque, and classical periods, the Jewish world was dark and shuttered. The Catholics were able to accomplish this by simply removing the second commandment.

The kosher laws are a curious collection of dietary restrictions. Among many others, they ban the mixing of milk and meat at the same table, they ban shellfish including lobster, clams, shrimp, and crabs. They ban birds of prey or scavenger, and a host of others. Often, the assertions made that these were ancient rules designed to protect the community from disease or other health problems. Most responsible scholars over the centuries hold however, that these laws are purely based on ritual and were not based on any sanitary principle.

The first example would be the mixing of milk and dairy. Ex 23:19, 23:26 and Deut 14:1. These actual words of the Torah merely state that a "kid" shall not be steeped in his mother's milk. This is a far cry from banning all meat with dairy. A kid is only the offspring of a goat and has nothing to do with the other kosher animals – cows, deer, sheep or bison. However, the interpreters of this law over the ages expanded it far beyond its original intention.

It has been suggested that the kid, since his mother was nursing, might have been too young, but most young goats were at least one year old before they would have served as a meat. It has also been suggested, that the pots in which the kid was steeped were made of copper which may have clashed chemically with the milk. None of these explanations has been found to hold water. Instead the prohibition must be seen as having only validity as a ritual.

Nothing is inherently wrong with a ritual which gives meaning to the practitioner. Often, it may give meaning or structure to a life and be invoking a discipline as an abstract way of worshipping or acknowledging God. It is interesting that many people with no interest in being religious by the practice of food rituals, do in fact observe stringent and often obscure dietary practices. These are occasionally published in one form or another. Diets for weight loss, vitamins, natural foods, or various minerals are often unproven, have claims which are unverified, and do little good other than to enrich the owners of the "nutraceutical" company which purveys it. Organic food, "free range" food, avoidance of genetically enhanced food, are areas where little or no benefit has been shown to be derived from it other than a reduction in the size of one's wallet. Yet people engage in the ritual of food selection. Eggs for example were considered dangerous just a few years ago, but are now considered a source of cheap wholesome protein.

Food rituals such as the kosher laws are probably a benign discipline which helps Jews to fulfill some of the many laws of their faith and thus are a form of worshipping God and sharing an identity with the Jewish community. To some, it simply feels right to practice kosher living. There is certainly no harm in that. The harm comes from the raising of sensible rules for governing one's daily life and service to the community to an excessive and ritualized level that exceeds practical benefits.

The handwashing ritual is another example. Obviously, it is necessary and healthy to wash one's hands after touching things that may spread disease. However, excessive ritualism attached to an otherwise common practice puts a stumbling block to reasonable daily functions that injects an unreasonable and unnecessary measure of guilt.

These doctrines and strong warnings against inter-faith marriage have caused the isolation and unnecessary mystification of Jewish religionists over the centuries.

These excessive insistences on proper ritual practice have had deleterious effects on Jews over the centuries. The Chasidim, with no biblical or Talmudic encouragement, have adopted nineteenth century ghetto clothing and grooming to set them apart from non-Jews. The enforced isolation of the Jewish communities by their own rules mysterious to the non-Jew, creates an aura of mistrust, and encourages unnecessary rumors perhaps none so pernicious as the infamous blood libel. The distance created continues today to provoke unnecessary enmity. The unfortunate effect is to associate solely the rituals such as Chasidic dress and kosher laws with Judaism rather than the beneficial doctrines it could bring to Western culture such as a devotion to rule by law, to education, to charity, to proper relations with those in commerce or with one's spouse, and women in general. The latter one highly prized in Judaism but not communicated adequately to the general public.